CREATION SCIENCE CLUB

# The Big Auger

John and Lisa Fox

**The Big Auger**
**The Creation Science Club: Book 4**
by John and Lisa Fox

First printing: January 2016


ISBN 978-1-942773-03-0
Cover design: BookFuel
Design and layout: BookFuel
Style and proofreading: Dr. Robert Carter and Lita Cosner



Published by:

CREATION
BOOK PUBLISHERS

**Creation Book Publishers**
P.O. Box 350
Powder Springs, GA, 30127, USA.
Phone: 1-800-616-1264
creationbookpublishers.com

We want to dedicate this book
to Lisa's sister, Kathi.
Kit-Kat—Thank you for teaching me to read,
and for telling us 10,000 exciting stories.
ljf

We also want to thank:

Buddy Davis, whose creation music ministry and dinosaur sculpting first inspired us to dig deeper into the truth,

Jonathan Sarfati, who has written books to refute the endless barrage of evolution's 'overwhelming evidence' coming at us from every side,

Creation Ministries International, for providing us all with various resources and an endless supply of 'scientific stones of truth' for our slings.

With special gratitude to Dr. Robert Carter, Lita Cosner, and others at CMI for taking the time to review this book.

*Note: If any errors or misuse of terms or facts
occur in this series, these mistakes are solely
the responsibility of the authors.

PART 1

# Radiometric Dating

# CHAPTER 1

*Slam!* Mike found himself pinned to the tavern wall by the rough hands of a giant. The Big Auger growled down into his face, "I asked you a question, Mikey…what ya doin' nosin' around my business?"

Nobody at the Hog's Den came to Mike's aid—anybody fool enough to make the Big Auger mad deserved whatever they got. Besides, it would've taken five men to hold Big Aug back, and there wasn't a man there that wanted to get on Aug's bad side.

Mike felt himself being lifted off the floor by the front of his jacket. He closed his eyes and cringed. "Hey, man. R-r-really, man. I don't know nothin'…nothin' about yer business."

*Slam!* Mike hit the wall again. "Yer a liar, Mikey. I hate liars. Now, tell me why you was nosin' around in my business or I'll flatten yer face."

Mike shuddered. "No, man…r-r-really, I ain't lyin'. I don't know nothin'. It was those guys, them two guys out there, that told me you was gonna lose yer land. I ain't been nosin' around in yer business. Ya gotta believe me, man."

Big Aug hesitated for a minute, then let Mike drop to the floor. The bartender sighed with relief, but most of the patrons looked disappointed. A good fight was always fun—not that Mikey would have lasted more than ten seconds.

"What men you talkin' about? And, what's they doin' lookin' into my business?"

Mike backed a few feet away. "Man…I don't know nothin'. All I know is that these two guys in some fancy ride told me they'd give me 50 bucks if-ins I got ya to go out and talk with 'em."

Aug took a menacing step closer to Mike. "And that's all they said?"

Mike wasn't about to look up into the Big Auger's face, so he just stared into the red eyes of the bull's head Aug had on a chain around his neck. "Uh…they jest said that they heard you was havin' trouble makin' payments. And they said if you'd do a favor fer 'em, they could make sure ya wouldn't lose yer land."

Aug turned away. "I ain't interested. Get lost."

Mike was either really dumb or really needed that 50 bucks, because he didn't leave. "Man, I ain't lookin' to get ya mad—no way, man. But, ya know, these fellows don't look like the usual kind that come 'round here. They got class. I mean, they're gonna give me 50 bucks jest fer gettin' ya out in the alley to talk with 'em—*50 bucks!"*

The Big Auger tightened his jaw as he considered what Mike had said. Finally, he dropped a ten-dollar bill on the bar and headed toward the side door—the door that led out to the alley.

*******

Hiking his way through a field thick with spring flowers, Aaron Franklin beat a shortcut up Maple Hill. At fourteen, Aaron stood just over six feet and planned on adding a few more inches. His friends called him *long and lean*. His older sister called him a *beanpole*.

Aaron was excited, and eager to get where he was going. But, as he approached a group of trees, his pace began to slow…until he came to a complete stop. Something wasn't right. It was too quiet. Looking nervously over his shoulder, he instinctively reached for his back pocket.

Suddenly, from both the left and the right, brightly colored objects were hurled straight toward him. Leaping backward, Aaron put his gun to work. Right, left; then, right again. As his ammo made contact, there were wet and messy explosions everywhere. Left, right, left. Backing up against a tree, Aaron continued to fight off the attack. Not once was he hit. Not once did he miss his target. Then, as suddenly as it had started, it was over. Carefully reloading his weapon, Aaron watched and waited.

After a few tense seconds, the branches in a tree just ahead began to rustle, and a voice called out from among the leaves. "No fair! You're a cheater-cheater-ice-cream-eater!" Darin Tadue swung down out of the tree, crossed his arms, and put on a disgruntled expression. "Twelve of Maniac Magazine's Super-Soaker water balloons all wasted! I don't think even one drop of water hit you."

Then, two other boys appeared from behind the bushes. Darin's identical twin, Abel, hurried over to shake Aaron's hand. "That was some mighty fine shootin' there, cowboy!"

And David Avila came over and swatted his friend on the arm. "Man, where did you ever learn to shoot like that?"

"Well," Aaron laughed, "when city life got kinda slow, Tasha and I used to play around a little with these pellet guns our parents got for us."

"'Used to play around a little'?" Darin snorted through his nose. "Yeah, right! Looks to me more like you went to Secret Agent Small Arms Academy."

David agreed. "Man! You were great! You gotta show me how to use that thing."

"Sure," Aaron smiled. "But, first…I'm starved. Didn't Mrs. Carmen promise she'd send a couple dozen cookies up with Billy?" He paused and looked at his friends suspiciously. "You guys better not've eaten 'em all."

"Well, you know the rules…" Darin shouted as he took off running toward a large cabin, "*winner takes all.*"

The others didn't wait around—Mrs. Carmen's cookies were too good to risk losing.

*******

Pushed up into the tree line of Maple Hill is the cabin and workshop of a small group of scientists and friends who call themselves the Creation Science Club. At the beginning of the school year, Billy James, along with Darin and Abel (the Tadue twins) had volunteered themselves as tutors for Darwin Middle School's eighth grade honors science class.

The start of this club was the start of a battle for the minds of Greenville. Being a small farm town, nearly all of Greenville's population had its roots in the Christian faith. However, over the past 25 years, the nearby college—Quantum Leap University—had been flexing its secular muscles, most notably in its many newspaper articles and frequently televised news reports on evolution. With its confident, smooth words and highfalutin language, evolution had begun nudging the written truths of the Bible out from the minds of the folks of Greenville.

Overall, the people's loss of faith in the basic truths of the Bible went unnoticed. And yet, God had kept a remnant whose faith in God's Word would not be swayed. These were the people who could see the change in those around them. They could see how a loss of trust in a few parts of the Bible had led to a loss of trust in the whole Bible. And, it was this loss of trust that was leading many of Greenville's citizens down a path of confusion and uncertainty. And, for many, the end of this path was a shipwrecked faith.

*******

After the gang had emptied two big plates of cookies and a gallon of milk, Billy put all the boys to work photographing and documenting the results of their latest experiment. But, David noticed that Billy seemed preoccupied. Instead of leading the boys in a fun, fact-filled conversation like usual, he just kept sighing and shaking his head.

Finally, David asked, "Uh…hey, Billy, is anything the matter? Mrs. James okay and all?"

Billy looked at David blankly for a second, then sighed again. "Don't worry, David, I'm fine. And, Carmen's fine, too." But then, he suddenly slapped the counter top in frustration. "It's just that I'm concerned about Dr. Ted and Dr. Ed's museum. Last night, someone broke in and set one of the storage rooms on fire. And, since the museum is still in transition, a lot of costly items were boxed up in there. Some of it's ruined beyond repair."

David could hardly believe it. He had just been at Dr. Veritas's museum a few days before. He had been one of the volunteers who had helped to safely pack up the displays until the previously secular museum could be transformed into a Creation Museum.

Aaron stopped what he was doing and walked over to Billy. "They saying it was arson?"

"Yep. Sheriff Murphy is sure," Billy answered while drumming his fingers on the counter. "He says all the clues point to Big Aug Cussler—he's a kinda local 'thug-for-hire.' Of course, for now, there's no proof. The point is that if Big Aug did the job, then someone hired him to do it. Someone…"

"…Someone who doesn't want to see a Creation museum open up in Greenville," David finished Billy's sentence.

"You got it," Billy agreed grimly. "Dr. Lution's planning to put in a new security system. But he's estimating that their losses in the fire will back up the opening of the museum by two to four months."

"I guess we shouldn't be so surprised," Abel commented in a frustrated tone, "I mean, considering all the negative garbage the news has been throwing out about Dr. Ted and Dr. Ed's Creation Museum plans."

"Yeah." Darin drew down his brows. "It's like, so weird. I think Channel 4 has only had Dr. Ted's little museum on their news once in the last year. But, in the last month, they've had it on the news five times."

"And," David put in, "they just keep talking about how his plans to make it into a *Creation Museum* are 'so controversial.'"

Aaron smirked. "I'll bet it wouldn't be 'so controversial' if the news folks hadn't decided to make it 'so controversial.'"

"Well," Billy said, "one thing's for certain—if the news folks are making such a big deal out of Dr. Ted's little museum, it must be because some pretty powerful people have decided they don't want to see a Creation Museum in Greenville."

# CHAPTER 2

"Dr. Eugene Filler states, 'Scientific methods date this fossil to be 10.4 million years old.'"

"Dr. Holly Gratiss explains, 'Radiometric dating shows this fossil to be 950,000 years old.'"

"Dr. John Alexander presents the facts, 'We know, through proven scientific dating methods, that this fossil is between 350 and 400 million years old.'"

David rolled his eyes as he rolled his chair back from the computer to check out the library entrance…again. Looking at his watch, he sighed and decided to take a little walk over to the library's wildlife section. It wasn't long before he'd found an interesting book about Amur (Siberian) tigers. But, as he headed back to his computer, he was caught off guard by an unusual sight. Taking a few steps back behind the bookshelves, he peeked through the empty spaces on the shelf.

Miss Abigail Informed (soon to be Mrs. Ted Veritas) was seated at a small table next to a large, rough-looking, but handsome enough, young man. Between them was a book. Miss Abbi read, "There are many kinds of spiders all over the world. Some are very big, but most are small. Some are very tiny." Then she turned to the big man. "Okay, it's your turn."

The man ran his fingers nervously through his longish hair. Then, after glancing around, he started, "Spiders might not be…c-cute or…cud-d-ly, but some p-p-people do keep them as pets." Miss Abbi praised him, and the man's face filled with a boyish smile. Then, they turned to the next page in their book.

After a moment's hesitation, David walked toward his librarian friend and her student. The man immediately stopped reading and gave him a dirty look. David would have turned on his heels and scooted out of there, but Miss Abbi called to him, "Hello, David. How's your research on radiometric dating going?"

David took a step closer to the table. "Pretty good, thanks. Dr. Nottah gave us a list of websites to review and four articles to read before tomorrow."

Miss Abbi seemed very comfortable seated next to the man who was at least twice her size. "David, I'd like you to meet a new friend of mine." And, turning to the man, she said, "This is Augustine. He's been coming to the library on his evenings off to practice his reading skills."

David looked the man in the eye and smiled, then held out his hand. The man seemed uncertain, but took David's hand. Everyone had to laugh as Augustine's giant hand *swallowed* David's.

With everyone more relaxed, David sat down. "Man, you sure got a lot of courage."

The man looked pleased with the compliment, but asked, "Why ja say that?"

"Well, you know, a lot of big guys like you, who have trouble reading, just keep on using their muscles to earn a living. I guess they'd rather 'die in the mines' than admit they can't read."

"See, I told you so," Abbi said, patting Augustine on the arm.

"Besides," David said, "just because you have trouble reading doesn't mean you're not smart. I mean, Albert Einstein had trouble learning to read. And he turned out to be one of the smartest people ever."

Abbi glowed. "Augustine, here, says he's always loved science, but had trouble with reading." Then, her face got sober. "In the third and fourth grade, the other kids teased him because he couldn't read yet. So, he just stopped trying." Miss Abbi screwed up her face and shook her fist as she continued, "Boy, if I could get hold of those kids, I'd spank their bottoms good and hard!"

Augustine chuckled. "Aw, Miss Abbi, them kids are all growed up now. Besides, I guess I already paid 'em back aplenty." For a moment, his face darkened. He got quiet and seemed uncomfortable. Then, he stood up rather suddenly and looked at David. "Good ta meet ya, kid." Then, he said to Abbi, "Thanks. I'll be back nex' Tuesday." And he turned and left.

David watched him go. "Man, the floor shakes when he walks!"

Miss Abbi laughed. "First time he came around here, you can bet I was nervous. After all, he is Big Aug Cussler."

*"The Big Auger?"* David was shocked. "But he's the guy Billy says the cops are blaming for the fire at Dr. Ted's museum."

Abigail turned pale and put her hand to her mouth. But then she straightened up. "That can't be! Augustine would never do such a thing! He loves museums. And, besides, he knows Ted and I are engaged."

"Well," David shrugged, "Billy was saying that people sometimes pay Big Aug to do their dirty work."

Miss Abbi sighed. "I know he's had a rough start in life. And he's even been arrested a few times. But, he says he's trying to start over. And I believe him."

"I hope you're right." David shook his head.

Just then, Jill and Jack Hill, and Aaron Franklin came rushing through the library doors. "Sorry we're so late," Jack called.

"Shush! Library voices!" Miss Abbi corrected him with a smile. The four teens giggled, then headed back to the computers. But Miss Abbi went straight to her desk and called Dr. Ted.

*******

Out in the library parking lot, David and Aaron waved goodbye to Jack and Jill as they left with their mom. "I can't believe we made it through all of Dr. Nottah's required reading." David shook his head vigorously, as if trying to clear it. "Talk about b-o-r-i-n-g. I mean—that was snooze-city."

"You really think so?" Aaron seemed surprised. "I think trying to date rocks and fossils and stuff is really cool."

David laughed. "You are such a geek! Even if you can smear me in basketball, you have to be a geek if you think radiometric dating is *fun*."

Aaron answered David by knocking him to the ground. And the match was on.

Five minutes later, when Billy and the Tadue twins pulled up, the boys were still at it. Billy laughed and beeped the horn. "Hey, you two, break it up! Your parents expect me to get you home in one piece."

As they hopped into the jeep, David explained in a taunting tone, "Aaron, here, thinks radiometric dating is 'cool.'"

Much to David's surprise, Darin reached out to meet Aaron in a knuckle-knock, while Abel exclaimed, "Nothing can be as cool as the science behind dating different materials!"

As he buckled up, David leaned his head back against his seat and rolled his eyes. "If you guys can convince me that radiometric dating is cool, I'll buy each of you your own super-sonic-sensational-strawberry sundae at Favorite Flavors."

"You're on!" Billy said. "Except, make mine blueberry."

*******

The next morning, bright and early, the members of the Creation Science Club were traveling along an old farm road. David, Aaron, and Darin were having a contest to see who could spot the most cats. Abel was keeping score.

"Black, short hair, white chest," David shouted out.

A minute later, "Orange tabby with two gray kittens!" Darin shouted. "Whoo-hoo! Look at me! I am *El Numero Uno*! That gives me an even ten. Just goes to show who's got the eagle eyes around here!"

"He might have eagle eyes," David commented to Aaron. "But he crows like my grandpa's old struttin' rooster."

"I heard that!" Darin accused. "You're just jealous because you've only seen four."

After about two hours, the boys had played *Count the Cats*, then *Count the Dogs*, then *License Plate Alphabet* three times, and they'd even resorted to singing *100 Bottles of Root Beer on the Wall.*

But, at long last, Billy pulled the jeep and its occupants into some sort of construction zone. Pointing over toward several steep cliffs, Billy explained, "This is a quarry—you know, where they dig out rock beds." Then he pointed to a tractor-trailer parked about 100 yards away. "And that over there is Dr. Katie Borton's research laboratory."

David looked surprised. "Dr. Borton? The lady who visited Galápagos with us? I thought her name was *Hope*."

Billy climbed out of the jeep and explained, "Dr. Katie is Dr. Hope's sister." Then he went on to say, "Scientists often like to come out when companies are making deep cuts into the earth. It's like free and easy access to a multitude of perfectly preserved rock layers." Billy grabbed a couple of bags of gear and tossed one to Abel, then one to Darin. "Dr. Katie and her brother, Dr. Stephen, have been taking rock samples from different layers and doing some radiometric dating of their own." Billy grabbed the last two bags for himself. "And, here's something Dr. Katie just told me—all the Bortons go to the same church as Dr. Nottah."

"No way!" Aaron said with a laugh. "Like, maybe they'll help Dr. Nottah become a Christian."

Billy stopped walking and said seriously, "You guys, it's not for us to say whether Dr. Nottah is a Christian or not. He says he is. And we should accept his testimony. You know, only God can see into the heart of a man." Then he smiled. "But one thing's for sure, their being in the same church didn't happen by chance. God's got a plan.

"Now, let's get moving. I promised Dr. Katie that we'd gather some samples for them before lunch."

*******

Suspended 50 feet down from the top of the sheer cliff, David looked over at Aaron, who was about three feet to his right, and smiled. Aaron looked down to the boulder-strewn ground below them and couldn't quite smile back. David was using a special tool that extracted rock samples out of the cliff wall. He would then put the sample in a specifically-marked bag and hand it to Aaron.

Darin and Abel were a few hundred feet up and over, recording everything with the super-zoom camera-mode on Darin's bionic binoculars. Dr. Katie wanted there to be no questions about the extraction location of each sample.

An hour later, as the boys were nearing the top of the cliff, Aaron had obviously forgotten his initial anxieties. Bouncing himself back and forth off the face of the rock wall, he urged David, "Come on, man, hurry up! Only two more samples and it's lunch time!" Then, settling down to hold a card by David as he drilled sample #22-75904, Aaron turned to ham it up for Darin's camera with a big smile.

*******

Back at the Borton's semi-trailer laboratory, lunch was over, and Dr. Katie and her brother, Dr. Stephen, were showing everyone how they did the initial testing on the rock samples.

"So," David summarized, "you guys test each of the samples in more than one way and see how the different results match up."

"That's right," Dr. Katie said. "Then, we also send a portion of the same samples over to Quantum Leap University for re-testing. Our sister, Hope, is overseeing those tests."

"Actually," Dr. Stephen broke in, "today's sample collections are just a repeat of what we did last month. There was some kind of 'supposed' mix-up at the QLU lab, and our last three weeks of tests were compromised."

Billy looked concerned. "What do you mean by 'supposed' mix-up?"

"Well, you've seen how careful we are to make sure everything is double, and even triple-checked—to make certain there aren't any mix-ups on samples, locations, dates, or test results." Then, looking at his sister and seeing her slight nod, Dr. Stephen continued. "Well, we can't prove anything, but it's starting to look like someone who has inside access at QLU is messing with our samples and data—purposely trying to make our results inconclusive."

"Why would they want to do that?" David wondered.

Darin spoke up, "It's like this, David-dude. According to evolution, the rock layers in these hills represent millions and millions of years. So, if an evolutionist took a rock sample from 50 feet down into the hill, and then another one 500 feet down into the hill, he would expect to find the sample from near the top to be millions of years *younger* than the sample way down low. But…"

"…But," Abel took over, "instead, new studies are putting relatively little time gaps between the widely separated layers."

Billy nodded, then turned to Dr. Stephen. "So, you're thinking that someone is trying to cover up the evidence against evolution by messing with your stuff."

"It certainly wouldn't be the first time evolutionists scrambled to cover up the shortcomings of their theory," Dr. Stephen said with a shrug.

"Well, anyway," Dr. Katie said in a more positive tone, "we have the *truth* on our side. Evolutionists can't hide behind a lie forever. Even with all their expensive 'advertising,' the truth is starting to shine through. It's just a matter of time before we take creation back from the evolutionists."

"Yahoo!" Darin and Abel shared a sting high-five. "It's a matter of fact, that we're taking creation back!"

Billy chuckled, then turned to the Bortons. "Now, Dr. Stephen and Dr. Katie, I need you guys to explain to David, here, how and why rock dating is so important and interesting. And," he added with a chuckle, "I'll thank you to make it as exciting as possible, since I have a blueberry super-sonic-sundae riding on it."

# CHAPTER 3

Dr. Chance Nottah's students sat in the semi-dark, intently watching the visual tours filling the screen at the front of the room. Awesome cinematography took the class into the very bowels of the sparkling diamond mines of Africa. Next, they were flying above the verdant cliffs of Venezuela. Finally, they were out on a glass overhang looking straight down into the spectacular Grand Canyon. It was all breathtakingly beautiful.

Monte Carlo, the ever-popular adventure movie hero, had been the video's tour guide. The girls giggled and sighed whenever Monte gave his signature lop-sided grin. The boys sat quietly, but mentally determined that one day their muscles would be as big as his. Everybody loved Monte. And, most of the students nodded as he made his concluding statement: "Diamond mines, beautiful cliffs, and awesome canyons all tell the same story—our amazing Earth is many hundreds of millions of years old."

Switching off the DVD player, Dr. Nottah faced his class of honors science students and began lecturing. "Radiometric dating is a proven scientific method for putting a near exact age on any given rock sample."

David's hand shot up into the air. Dr. Nottah rolled his eyes, but asked, "What is your question, David?"

"Well, sir," David began politely, "from the articles you assigned, I understand that dating rocks isn't actually, well... isn't measuring a real date."

Dr. Nottah's face tightened, and the rest of the class could feel the tension in the room rising. "What is your point, David?"

"Well, sir," David explained, "it seems radiometric dating isn't really measuring the *date* of a rock, it's actually measuring certain *elements* within the rocks."

Click, click, click. Dr. Nottah started snapping his thumbnails together—a sure sign, the class had quickly learned, that he was irked. "That's right, David—*very accurate* measurements."

"Yes, very accurate," David responded. "And, I understand that scientists use the ratios of these different elements to determine the age of the rocks."

"Correct, correct." Dr. Nottah nodded and visibly relaxed, and the whole class seemed to breathe easier. Dr. Nottah explained, "In the rocks we are dating, there is a starting element, called the *parent* element. And then there is another element that is the result of the *parent* element's decay, called the *daughter* element. Scientists are able to accurately measure the ratio between the *parent* element and the *daughter* element. The age of the rock is then determined by this ratio."

"But, sir," David said in a perplexed tone, "while I see that an accurate *ratio* can be measured, I don't understand how this gives an accurate *date*."

Dr. Nottah gave the seemingly obvious answer. "The accurate ratios tell how much of the *parent* element has decayed, and therefore, allowing an accurate age of the rock to be determined."

"But, without knowing how much of the *parent* element was in the rock to begin with, the ratio doesn't really mean anything." David continued, "And, the assigned readings never really explained how scientists know how much of the *parent* element is in the rock to begin with."

Dr. Nottah hesitated, then replied, "These are good questions, David. I can tell that you're really thinking this through. Now, to answer your question: Scientists take a similar rock of a known age and carefully measure its *parent/daughter* ratio. Then, they compare it to the rock of an unknown age to come up with an accurate date."

"I see," David said.

Dr. Nottah looked relieved, but David wasn't done. "But sir, how do they know for certain the age of that rock they compared with the rock of an unknown age?"

"Well, David..." Dr. Nottah slowed down, being careful to give the best possible answer, "scientists can use *index fossils* found in the rock layers to help determine the age of the surrounding rocks. If the fossil is a million years old, the rock surrounding it is also a million years old."

"So, how do they know the age of these index fossils?"

Dr. Nottah closed his eyes and gave the answer his professors had given him. "By comparing these index fossils to the age of the surrounding rocks that..." Dr. Nottah suddenly stopped. He drew down his brows, realizing he was backing himself into the corner of circular reasoning. Clicking his thumbnails several times, he continued, "Ummm...by... well, comparing them to the surrounding rocks that have been dated using radiometric dating techniques."

"You mean more *parent/daughter* ratio comparisons of different rocks?" David asked.

The cornered principal looked hopefully at the clock on the wall—still five minutes of class left. "Yes..." he said slowly. "I suppose that's what I mean."

By this time the class was hardly breathing, waiting for the outcome of this duel.

"But then, how could an age be placed on those ratios? I mean, you just keep going from rock to rock, or rock to fossil, or from fossil back to rock. There has to be an *original* rock somewhere, right? Well, how did they come up with an accurate age for that original rock?"

Click, click, click. "David," Dr. Nottah sighed, "I respect your desire to learn. But…I'm afraid I can't take the time to explain all these things at the present. Class is nearly over… and…I need to assign your next reading."

A few of the students in the class kept their eyes straight toward Dr. Nottah as he wrote their assignment on the board. But most of the kids turned and smiled at David—the clear winner of the duel.

*******

With a low, guttural growl, the 12-foot Siberian tiger followed the warm trail of its prey. Each of its paws left massive prints—pressed deep into the soft earth by the giant cat's 800-plus pounds. On its forehead it wore the famed Chinese Wang mark, which crowned it king of the world. Up ahead, the long-legged deer sprinted to keep as wide a gap as possible between itself and certain death.

After a short chase, the tiger paused, seeming to sense that speed would not earn it this meal. Looking around for a place to conceal itself, the powerful cat spotted a rocky outcrop of large boulders. Crouching down, it found an opening among the rocks. Going further back, the tiger discovered a tunnel. Advancing silently into the tunnel, the tiger saw that it opened up into some sort of large den or small cave. The tiger smiled at its discovery. Then, turning around, it crawled back out. Bounding excitedly along the path in the woods, the huge cat let out a long, loud roar. In response to its roar, the fleeing deer unexpectedly turned and ran back toward the tiger.

Then, just as the deer and the tiger were about to meet, a mighty hunter appeared on the path. Lowering his large-game rifle, he raised his hand and removed his sunglasses. "Sorry, guys," Darin told the others. "No more hunting today. Abel just called and said Billy needs us down at the cabin right away. There's been more trouble at Dr. Teddy's museum."

David and Aaron removed their own *Reality Morphing* glasses, and they all headed down Maple Hill.

*******

At the museum, Dr. Ted Veritas, Dr. Edward Lution, and Miss Abbi Informed were talking to the policeman in charge. "But, officer," Miss Abbi was saying, "I've been working with him for the last several weeks. I can't believe that he'd be responsible for this."

The policeman kept a professional face. "M'am, I understand that you want to believe that the Big Auger's turned over a new leaf. But, his reputation's speaking out against him. He's a well-known troublemaker. And, not just his reputation, but the facts are talking pretty loudly right now. We've got more than one mug shot of Big Aug down at the station. And, in each shot, he's wearing a chain with the head of a bull on it."

"What's going on?" Billy quietly asked Dr. Lution.

Dr. Lution sighed. "Well, someone broke into the museum—in spite of the new alarm system—and stole some things…and accidentally left something behind. It's a broken chain with the head of a bull on it."

"Oh, no!" David clenched his fists. "Then it *was* the Big Auger!"

*******

A few days later, David, Aaron, and his sister, Natasha, were sitting around a campfire close to the pond at Billy and Carmen's place—ErinWood. Abel and Darin were stealthily stalking a large Luna moth they'd seen fly by as dusk had set in. Abel had decided it would make an impressive gift for Aaron's sister, Tasha.

As the fire flickered, Billy was leaning contentedly against an old stump with Mrs. Carmen dreamily resting on his shoulder.

Suddenly, Billy let out a holler and jumped to his feet. Untucking his shirt-tails, he hopped up and down. Aaron and David also jumped to their feet, wondering what was wrong. But, Mrs. Carmen just whooped a mischievous laugh.

*"Ice cube!* That woman snuck an ice cube down my collar!" Billy accused.

"Aw," Mrs. Carmen laughed. "I was just getting you back for that cute little toad I found on my pillow last night."

Billy tried to look innocent. "I don't know what you're talkin' about!" But it was obvious he was guilty.

"We're even now," Mrs. Carmen smiled, "so, you can sit down." Still, Billy hesitated. So she held up her empty hands. "See, no more ice." Then, she added with mock innocence, "Don't you trust me?"

"Yeah, right," Billy said, taking his seat. "I trust you about as much as Samson trusted Delilah."

Everyone laughed, but Aaron's curiosity was roused. "I thought Samson was the strongest man ever—why would he be afraid of a girl?"

Billy kissed his wife gently on the cheek and winked at Tasha. "Boy, you'd better watch out. Girls can be *more* than a match for any man. Don't ever underestimate a girl. Samson did, and he paid for it."

Aaron looked doubtful. "I think I need to hear the story again to believe that."

"Besides," Tasha added, "I thought Samson and Delilah loved each other."

Mrs. Carmen leaned forward. "It happened like this... Samson was born during a time of trouble and confusion in Israel. They had no king, and they sure weren't being faithful to God. Plus, the Philistines were continually terrorizing them. So, God sent a very special person to help the Israelites—Samson. Now, you'd think he would have been a pure, honest, fearless leader for his people. But, instead, he grew up to be a selfish, impure man who lived a violent life. His purpose seemed to be to terrorize the enemy who had terrorized his own people."

Billy nodded sadly. "Yep, to hurt and to maim was Samson's favorite game."

"So," Aaron prompted, "where does Delilah come in?"

Mrs. Carmen shrugged. "I guess she and Samson did love each other in a way—but not in a good way. Remember, Delilah was a Philistine. The Philistines hated Samson. So, they basically told Delilah, 'Find out what makes Samson so strong, or we'll kill you.' Now, Delilah was just as selfish and impure as Samson. So, she teased and begged and complained and whined until Samson finally told her his secret. Then she handed him over to the Philistines."

"So," Aaron summarized, "it wasn't strength, but *nagging* that destroyed the strongest man in the world."

David had a serious look on his face. "Billy, what you guys said about Samson makes me think of Big Aug Cussler—'To hurt and to maim was Samson's favorite game.' Miss Abbi said that they've put out a warrant for Big Aug's arrest."

"I guess Samson was even more of a trouble maker than the Big Auger is," Aaron joked. "I'm guessing the Philistines had a bunch of warrants out for Samson's arrest."

"I'll bet you're right," Billy agreed. But then, he added more seriously, "Just like God was behind much of what

Samson did—well, a *very different someone* has to be behind what Big Aug is doing. It bothers me to think that someone is going to so much trouble to keep Dr. Ted's Creation Museum from opening."

Aaron looked into the fire for a minute, then said, "I don't know if I buy the theory that someone is trying to keep Dr. Ted's museum from opening. I think, maybe, Big Aug likes Miss Abbi and is just jealous of Dr. Ted. I mean, it's just a little museum. And, Greenville is, like, in the middle of nowhere. Who, with any weight behind him, is going to waste his time trying to keep it from opening?"

"I see where you're coming from, Aaron," Billy said. "But other creation museums have been opening around the country, and it seems that all sorts of folks with lots of 'weight behind them' have been giving these museums all the grief they can, trying to keep them from opening."

"You're kidding!" Tasha gasped.

"Nope, it's true," David responded. "My dad says that it has to do with John 3:19—people hate the light because it exposes their evil deeds. And, he said that their fear just proves how little faith they really have in evolution—in spite of all their big claims and fancy talk."

"Well," Aaron mused, "then maybe Big Aug is hanging out with Miss Abbi just to try and get some inside information."

*******

That night, David found himself in Dr. Ted's museum. He was alone, and it was dark. Hearing a noise, he headed toward the back storage room. Every nerve in his body told him that someone was hiding just around the next corner. He was petrified. He broke into a cold sweat. But still, he walked on.

Rounding the corner, David found himself face-to-face with the Big Auger. Well, not exactly face-to-face. Big Aug was towering over him, sneering down with a twisted smirk on his face. And, around his neck hung the chain with a silver bull's head. As David looked at the bull, its eyes shot fire out toward him. David tried to jump back, but Big Aug's giant hand thrust out and grabbed him around the throat.

"You ain't goin' nowheres, ya punk!" Then he laughed a deep, throaty laugh and said, "To hurt and to maim was the Big Auger's favorite game…"

David struggled and kicked, but Big Aug's hand only tightened around his throat.

Gasping and choking, David woke up to find his sister's cat—Lumpy—asleep across his neck. Pushing the fat cat off his bed, David rubbed his neck and shuddered. He certainly hoped the police had caught Big Aug.

# CHAPTER 4

## Radiometric Dating
## (Confirming Billions of Years?)

by David J. Avila

### Introduction

The theory of evolution claims that all of the life forms we see today (including humans) evolved from "the first single-celled organism." For this to be true, the earth would need to be billions of years old in order to allow enough time for the huge amount of genetic change necessary to enable this to happen. Evolutionists use various dating methods to support their belief that the earth is billions of years old. For this report, I will consider some of evolution's *best* dating methods and show that the evidence does *not* scientifically support billions of years. Rather, the evidence makes better sense when we interpret it according to what the Bible says—that God created the earth (and all life) about 6,000 years ago.

### Rock Layers

Evolutionists decided over 200 years ago (before modern scientific dating methods were invented) that the earth is billions of years old. The QLU website states, "No person has lived through deep time [billions of years], but we *know* it has occurred." Actually, they cannot "know" this for certain. It is simply the *assumption* they have chosen to believe.

Scientists first claimed to "know" that the earth is billions of years old based on the multitude of fine layers found in sedimentary rock all over the earth. Their assumption that the vast thicknesses of rock layers represent billions of years is based on their belief that rock layers form very slowly over millions of years. But this is not operational science—millions of years cannot be observed or tested. Rather, it is historical science—a belief about the past based on current evidence.

Operational science, however, has shown that fine-layered sediment can (under the right conditions) form very quickly. In one repeatable experiment, small particles that were allowed to settle under running water (at various speeds) produced a multitude of fine layers. But the eruption of Mount St. Helens is a much more impressive example. This volcanic explosion produced *25 feet* of fine-layered sediment in just a few hours. This observable science discredits evolution's interpretation of the evidence.

In fact, a closer look at the sedimentary rock layers themselves brings to light serious evidence against billions of years. Simple observation shows that there is a lack of erosion between rock layers supposedly separated by many millions of years. How could some layers not experience any erosion for millions of years? There is also a lack of disturbances within some rock layers. How could these layers wait millions of years to harden without worms or bugs or roots causing obvious disturbances? Scientists also regularly find polystrate fossils, which are fossils that pass through several rock layers vertically. Now, how could an animal or plant wait millions of years to be covered slowly-and-gradually by rock layers without first decaying?

Operational science verifies that millions of years are *not* needed in order to form vast layers of sedimentary rock. In fact, most of the current evidence refutes evolution's billions of years. It makes better sense to believe what the Bible says—that the earth is only thousands of years old, and that most of the rock layers were laid down quickly by a worldwide Flood.

**Radiometric Dating**

Evolutionists also use various radiometric dating methods to support their belief that the earth is billions of years old. These methods use element ratios as the foundation of their results. Some elements, like uranium (parent element), undergo radioactive decay to produce other elements (daughter element). Scientists can accurately measure the ratio of the amount of the *parent* element in a rock to the amount of the *daughter* element in a rock. They claim to be measuring the age of a rock, but actually, they are not measuring dates. They're just measuring element ratios.

To get supposed 'dates' from such measurements, a lot of *big* assumptions have to be made. First of all, evolutionists assume billions of years of history have passed. Then, they assume they are correct in their estimate of how much of the parent element was in the rock to begin with—billions of years ago. Next, they assume that the rate of decay has always been constant—over billions of years. Finally, they assume that none of the elements were lost from or added to the rock being measured—for billions of years. These are all big assumptions and a billion years is a very, very long period of time to 'assume' anything.

Evolutionists begin with these huge, billion-year assumptions, yet still confidently claim to 'know' that the rocks they are testing are billions of years old, therefore 'confirming' their original assumption that the *earth* is billions of years old.

## Radiometric Dating's Lack of Reliability

A certain primate skull fossil was discovered and brought in to be dated. The lab received an initial radiometric date of 230 million years. Evolutionists 'knew' this date was way off the mark because (they have decided) humans weren't around that far back. *Several* attempts were made at re-dating this fossil until they finally reached a more acceptable result of 2.9 million years. But, this was still a little too old according to their *belief* about human evolution. Further 'investigation' brought the radiometric age down to about 1.9 million years. Ah, just as they had expected all along—how convenient. This is just *one* example of how evolutionists have been 'working' the data until they find a date they 'know' is true. Is it really science to know your conclusion before the testing has even begun?

One rock from Mount St. Helens was known to be formed in 1986 (that's younger than my mom), but was dated to be 350,000 years old. Also, radiometric dates derived from five different lava flows from Mount Ngauruhoe in New Zealand ranged in age from 0.27 to 3.5 million years. But, in reality, all five lava flows had occurred within the last 50 years. Evolutionists 'explain' that excess argon from the magma was trapped in the rock when it solidified, making it test older than it really is. But, if we can't trust radiometric dating for rocks of known ages, how can we trust it for rocks of unknown ages? Who's to say that excess argon wasn't trapped in other rocks?

A rock sample from near the top of the Grand Canyon should be billions of years younger than a rock from near its bottom, according to evolution. However, an upper-layer rock was dated 270 million years *older* than a rock from the bottom layer. The evolutionists were defensive about these results. They claimed that if they had known the rock was from the upper level, the dates would have been measured differently and a correct date could have been given. But this makes no sense. Evolutionists shouldn't have to know how old a rock is before they test how old the rock is.

Evolutionists (and the media) present radiometric dating as a scientifically accurate way to determine the age of rocks. But the truth is, it's based on unprovable assumptions and often gives unreliable results.

## Other Evidence

Creationists are scientifically observing sound evidence that supports their belief that the earth is *not* billions of years old. (1) The rate of decay of the earth's magnetic field shows that it shouldn't be much more than about 10,000 years old. (2) The rate at which the moon is slowly receding away from the earth shows that it is much younger than evolutionists' claim of 4.6 billion years. (3) Currently, salt is entering the sea much faster than it is escaping—the sea is not nearly salty enough for this to have been happening for billions of years. (4) Radioactive decay releases helium into the atmosphere, but the total amount of helium in the atmosphere today is only about 0.05%. If this had been happening for billions of years, that number should be many, many, many times higher. All of this *scientific* evidence, and more, supports the idea that the earth is not billions of years old, but only thousands of years old.

## Conclusion

The theory of evolution claims that all of the life forms we see today (including humans) evolved from "the first single-celled organism." For this to be true, the earth would need to be billions of years old. However, various ways of estimating the age of the earth do *not* support the belief that the earth is billions of years old.

Operational science has shown that rock layers can form very quickly—requiring only hours or days, not billions of years. And radiometric dating is not the same as reading a calendar that shows the earth is billions of years old. Rather, it is based on unprovable assumptions, and it has shown, in many cases, to give extremely inaccurate information.

Creationists date the earth by using the history recorded in the Bible. They believe it is an accurate, eyewitness account of world history. And, more and more scientific data agrees with the biblical age of the earth. Evolutionists hold on to their belief that the earth is billions of years old and that evolution is true. But the evidence makes better sense when we start with what the Bible says, that God created the earth (and all life) about 6,000 years ago.

*******

**TO: moore-power@administration.qlu.net**
**FROM: chance@science.qlu.net**
**CC: hope@science.qlu.net**
**RE: Darwin Middle School**

**Dr. Moore-Power,**
**I cannot hide the fact that I feel unduly misused by you and the Board at QLU by being placed as principal and teacher here at DMS. I feel it is ridiculous to put a man of my learning and accomplishment in charge of pubescent children. However, since I pride myself in always doing things well, I have determined to do even this job well.**

**The students in my honors science class are very advanced in their desire to learn. If they were only graduate students at QLU, rather than 13- and 14-year-olds, I could quite enjoy working with them.**

However, as Dr. Edward Lution described back in February, there is an obvious mutiny within the class. Several children appear to be Christian fanatics of some sort. They refuse to accept evolution as a plausible theory. They won't accept any science—no matter how well founded—unless it agrees with what is written in the Bible.

I had decided to basically ignore these creationists—thinking that the more diligently they researched the facts in order to disprove evolution, the more evidence for evolution they would find. But, after reading through their reports, I have decided that I must address some of the issues they have raised. However, as my degree is not in geology, I don't feel that I can adequately respond to these specific issues. I have, therefore, forwarded a copy of David Avila's science report to the assistant director of the Geology Dept. at QLU (Dr. Hope Borton) for some clear answers.

PART 2

# Observable Speciation

# CHAPTER 5

The pack of cold-blooded reptiles silently slipped into the waters, their long bodies barely making a ripple. The frantic splashing of potential prey put the beasts into a nearly hypnotic state of anticipation. At up to 20 feet of bone-crushing muscle, these kings of the lake felt no need to watch their own backs as they prepared the ambush. The prey was common enough... small, long-legged mammals with big eyes and long lashes.

The group of predators submerged as one, gliding into the camouflage of the reeds. Looking through the cattails, the beasts considered their prey: delicate and defenseless. They must also be brainless… why else would they enter the waters ruled by the great Leviathan? Re-submerging, the monsters swam closer, closer, closer… Then, with a rush, they shot out of the water with their mouths open wide—fire roaring up and out of their throats.

*Splat!* One leviathan flew backwards, frantically scraping its claws along its long snout. Dark smoke drifted from its nostrils as it sputtered and coughed. The other two creatures heard their friend's distress but were already committed to the attack. *Schmoocck!* Great gobs of green goo squelched their fire and blinded them. *Sploot!* They shook their heads back and forth in confusion. And, by the time they had freed their faces of the balls of slimy pond scum, the delicate, defenseless mammals were out onto to the safety of the beach... laughing at them.

"You boys think you're so smart," Jill shouted, shaking her head with a smirk. "But you're just askin' for trouble when you start messin' with the girls."

"Yeah," Tasha added as she high-fived Cory, "You best just watch your back this weekend—you're up against brains, intuition, and ingenuity."

*******

Outside Billy's place, everyone chatted and laughed around a towering stack of sandwiches and a giant bowl of apple slices. Billy and Carmen were sponsoring a weekend camp out up at ErinWood. All the friends of the Creation Science Club had been invited. This would be the Soure family's last week in the States before returning to Argentina to continue their work as fossil-finders.

"That was Dad," Rebekah Soure told everyone as she snapped her cell phone shut. "He and Mom are on their way over." Sitting down next to Darin, she continued, "I guess Argentina rejected our appeal to have full control over our dino-eating mammal fossil. They did, however, agree that two people from our side of the issue will always be present whenever anything is done with it."

Abel was busy pouring Tasha a glass of lemonade, but paused long enough to say sarcastically, "That's very 'kind' of them."

Darin rolled his eyes as he added a fourth layer to his graham cracker and marshmallow creme layered desert, complete with M&M's. "Yeah. How 'kind' of them to let us watch *their* research on *our* discovery."

"Anyway," Stephen Soure (a.k.a. Stego) said as he reached for the jar of marshmallow creme, "at least they've agreed to *do* the research. The evolutionists were pushing to have it locked up in some 'never see the light of day' warehouse."

Darin scoffed, contemplating the best way to tackle his s'more creation, "They're just scared it might turn out to be the real thing."

Billy laughed at the results of Darin's first bite, then shook his head. "I'm guessing they'll have plenty to say no matter what the research results are. Evolutionists are not going to give up their millions of years that easily."

"A lot depends on how the media decides to carry it," Jack pointed out.

"Yeah," Aaron smirked. "But I wouldn't expect much support from that corner."

"I can see it now," David said. *"Creationists once again reject all factual science to believe a fairy tale."*

"You would think," Jack said, "that the media would at least take the time to really look at both sides of the issue. They've obviously already chosen the winner—even before the race begins."

Suddenly, Mrs. Carmen busted out laughing in response to something Jill had whispered in her ear. Tasha and Cory looked away, whistling innocently.

Billy looked over at the boys. "You all best watch yourselves. If the girls have my Carmen on their side, you're as good as goners. Believe me, I'm speaking from experience."

"No worries, guys!" Darin announced, unaware of the M&M marshmallowed to the end of his nose. "The girls don't stand a chance with *Darin the Invincible* on your team!"

Bekah slipped her arm through Darin's and sweetly plucked the M&M off his nose. But, before she led him off for a walk around the pond, David saw her wink at Cory. Unconsciously, he hiked his shorts a little higher.

*******

That night, David woke to the sound of sirens passing by. He rolled over in his sleeping bag and prayed quietly as his mother often did, "Lord, please protect whoever it is who's in need of help."

Then, looking up into the tree branches stretched out above him, David listened to the nearby frogs singing spring's serenades. In the distance, he heard another siren coming closer. As it passed by, David rolled over again, wondering what might be going on. A fire? An accident?

As the third siren approached and passed, three words flashed into David's mind: *the Big Auger*. Everyone knew that there was a warrant out for his arrest. And the police seemed convinced he was still somewhere around town. Maybe they had found him. That would be a relief.

Rolling over one more time, David realized that his second root beer float was not going to let him get back to sleep. So, he stood up and stretched his back. Then he quietly stepped over Aaron and Jack, heading off to the left side of the camp (the girls were to the right side). At the far edge of the camp, David passed Darin who was asleep beside his latest invention—a *scat the cat and scare the bear woodsmen's best friend.* It was, in reality, a medium-sized remote controlled robot that flashed bright lights and made loud noises to scare off any curious bears or bobcats. Darin had made a matching pair. The other WBF (woodsmen's best friend) was in the girls' camp. Bekah had the remote to that one.

After going a ways into the woods, David wished he had grabbed his flashlight. Oh well. No big deal. However, on his way back to camp, David started to feel kinda creeped out. He slowed down and glanced over his shoulder. Stego's goofy campfire ghost story suddenly seemed believable. Just a few more steps, he told himself, and he should be in sight of the camp. David hurried forward. No camp. Running his fingers through his already ruffled hair, he tried to get his bearings. Stay calm, he told himself.

*Crack!* A stick snapped. David looked toward the sound and saw something big lurking in the darkness. Panic ran through him like a lightning bolt. But, just as quickly, the fear drained back out of him. *Duh.* It had to be Cory or one of the girls. They probably had Abel's night-vision camcorder—just waiting to catch his terrified expression on film. Well, he would show them!

Hunkering down, David slunk behind a tree. As silent as a cat, he went from tree to tree until he could slip behind a thick group of bushes. There he sat, waiting. With each breath, his smile got bigger. Man, he was sure going to scare whoever was following him.

He could hear the footsteps coming closer. They seemed hesitant and uncertain. Closer. David tensed his muscles and got ready to spring. The instant he saw a foot step in front of the bush, he leaped—jumping straight up. But, just as he started to yell, "Got ya!" his voice caught in his throat. Through the dark shadows, he made out the silver head of a bull right in front of his face. Instinctively, he turned to run. But, a huge claw of a hand shot out and caught him around the mouth. Extreme power pulled him back against the solid wall of a huge man's chest—Big Aug Cussler.

# CHAPTER 6

David woke up to six faces looking down at him. Then, out of the corner of his eye, he saw a canteen of water tipping forward. Abel was ready to revive him the good old-fashioned way. David sat up like a shot. "Hey, I'm awake. Look! See, I'm awake."

Darin shook his head. "Man, David-dude, you okay? Mom says I can sleep through anything. But even I can't sleep through a WBF's bear-back-off alarm."

David rubbed his eyes and yawned.

Billy ruffled his hair. "Well, they always say teenagers sleep like logs."

Aaron helped David up off his sleeping bag, then said in a no-nonsense tone, "Mrs. Carmen and Mrs. Soure just called to say breakfast is up. If you're not ready in ten seconds, we're leaving without you."

Jack started the count down, "nine…eight…seven…"

*******

After breakfast, everyone saddled up a horse. David was the last one done. "Man, David," Cory commented, "if you don't stop yawning, you'll strain your jaw muscles. And, what happened? You look like you've got a fat lip."

"I'm fine," David said. Reaching up, he touched his lip and winced. "I just bumped it last night in the dark."

Billy maneuvered his Appaloosa into the middle of the group. "The early morning news is squawking about the bigwigs over at QLU having a huge press conference today. I guess they're finally going to unveil their latest 'proof' for evolution."

"They probably waited till Saturday just so they could be on the front page of the big Sunday paper," Bekah surmised.

"Man, they sure don't miss an opportunity for publicity," Stego complained.

"Well, I guess we'll hear plenty about it soon enough," Terry Soure said. "So, let's not let it ruin our fun today."

As the whole group spread out, David leaned over to tell Jack and Aaron, "Hey, guys, I left something back at ErinWood. Tell the others I'll meet you all up on Maple Hill. I'll take the short cut—I've been that way a hundred times."

"Need someone to go back with you?" Aaron volunteered.

"Thanks, man, but I'm fine," David said, as he turned his pony around.

*******

It was nearly 11:00 before David caught up again with the others. They were already inside the Maple Hill cabin with their horses tied out front. Sliding off his own pony, David took a second to gaze thoughtfully up into the woods behind the cabin. Then he stretched his tired muscles and headed in.

Inside, the front room was crowded. Everyone was up close to the computer, listening to the latest news.

"Now for the breaking news," the anchorman said in a serious tone. "Greenville's own Sheriff Shane Murphy has confirmed that he and four deputies chased Big Aug Cussler down Pike's Way and past Ol' Yeller Hill. The chase took place a little after midnight last night. However, when the Big Auger abandoned his vehicle near Tiller's Hill and took to foot, the lawmen lost his trail. Sheriff Murphy, however, seems sure that Big Aug is still in the area and urges citizens to contact his office with any information. The Big Auger is to be considered armed and dangerous."

Everyone in the room stayed quiet, even as the anchorman changed to a story about a new grocery chain moving into Greenville. Finally, Billy said, "Seein' how Tiller's Hill is right close to ErinWood, I think the girls better sleep inside for the rest of the weekend. And, I guess Terry and I can sleep in the work shed with the boys."

"Oh, come on!" David spoke up. "I don't think it's so dangerous. Besides, it sounds awful to have to sleep in the work shed—that's hardly camping out."

Aaron chimed in, "David's right. And, on top of that, Darin and Abel have been working on that animatronic dino display for Dr. Ted's museum. There's stuff *everywhere*."

"I'm not so sure camping out is such a good idea anymore," Jill said nervously. "I mean, this Big Aug thing kinda has me creeped out."

"You're just chicken," Jack started to tease his sister.

But, Dinah Soure broke in, "Then, I guess I'm chicken, too. The news said to consider Big Aug *armed and dangerous*. And," she added seriously, "there's no telling what a desperate man will do."

Nobody wanted to call off their fun weekend, but everyone knew only a fool puts himself in danger in the name of fun. So, everyone just looked around, hoping someone would come up with a good idea. It turned out that Tasha was that *someone*.

"I know," Tasha jumped up. "Why don't we camp out here at the Maple Hill Cabin? I mean, it's closer to town than ErinWood. I'm sure the Big Auger won't head *this* way. And, besides, Aaron and I can bring Aztec. Jack and Jill can bring Dodger. And, Billy can bring Arby and Rax. That way, we'll have four watchdogs. No one could get by that many dogs."

Billy and Carmen looked at each other, then at Terry and Dinah Soure. All four of the grownups thought it through and then smiled. "Good idea, Tasha!" Billy said. "We can camp right up behind the cabin on that flat area by the old meat shed."

Just then, Abel sounded a quick whistle. "Hey, everyone, looks like QLU is on the news." Everyone turned and focused on the computer screen.

A sharply dressed woman reporter held a microphone in front of the science building at Quantum Leap University. "This is Jeane Jennings, with GMM news, live at the QLU BioTech building. Dr. Nate Selekson and Professor Donna Taque have just finished the press conference on their latest extraordinary scientific findings. Nearly 500 teachers, students, and citizens were in attendance. Phil Lovit is down in the crowd getting people's reactions. Let's go to him now—live."

The screen picture changed to a casually dressed man standing among a milling crowd of people. Phil Lovit approached a young woman who looked like a college student. "Excuse me, miss, can you tell me what your reaction is to Dr. Selekson's scientific findings?"

The girl giggled when the mike was put close to her face. "Well, um, I don't know…I mean, what's the big deal? These guys take a bunch of field mice and breed them into desert mice. I mean, don't people do that all the time with dogs—like, breed them together to make a new kind of dog that acts the way they want them to?"

Phil seemed to feel the need to explain the significance of the experiment's results to the young woman. "Well, it is my understanding that the elite scientists here at QLU were using highly advanced technology to produce and document the making of a completely *new* species—that they were, in fact, documenting *evolution in action*."

"Oh, wow," the girl said, looking a bit confused.

The reporter then approached a middle-aged looking man. In response to Phil's prompting, the man drew down his eyebrows thoughtfully. "Well, I'm no scientist…but I guess the research speaks for itself. I'm so impressed with the amazing advancements that scientific study is making in our understanding of the world around us. I mean, if those guys can produce a whole new species of mouse in less than three years, there's no telling what Mother Nature could have created over the past 300 million years."

Phil nodded and smiled. "Yes, Mother Nature is indeed a wonderful creator."

A young man with long wavy locks and a scruff of a beard cut in. "Hey, Mother Nature isn't the Creator, God is! I don't believe a word of what they said. I think evolution is a bunch of garbage."

Phil seemed to enjoy the man's response. "So," he asked, "are you saying that you think this research was all a hoax?"

"Well, no, man," he replied in a subdued tone. "I just don't believe in evolution."

"But," Phil pushed, "Dr. Selekson and Professor Taque and their team just documented the change of one species of animal into a brand new species. Isn't that evolution?"

"Um, I don't know. I'm not a scientist. But, I am a Christian, and the Bible says God made the animals. It wasn't evolution, and it wasn't Mother Nature, either."

"So," Phil got in the young man's face, "are you denying that Mother Nature allows things to adapt and change to better fit their environment?"

"Well, no," the man said. "I mean, I'm not sure."

Phil tried not to roll his eyes as he turned back to face the camera. "Well, Jeane, it seems that Dr. Selekson's results are making everyone look a little more deeply at what they believe. Overall, I can only say that, no matter what people *believe,* they can't argue with the *facts.*"

By the time Phil Lovit had given the camera back to Jeane Jennings, Darin was up on the coffee table in the cabin. "Hey, Phil-man!" he taunted, "Why don't you come and ask me what I think? I've got some answers. I'll give you the *facts*!"

Rebekah shook her head and smiled a sad sort of smile. "Darin, we know that *you* have the answers. It's just that 90% of the rest of the world *doesn't.* They just keep on having to soak up what the media feeds them—and the media feeds them *evolution.*"

Cory spoke up in a loud, frustrated voice. "You can't believe how many times I hear people in my college classes talking about Christians 'cramming the Bible down people's throats' or 'brainwashing the children with religious junk.' But it's just the opposite. It's the evolutionists that are cramming their beliefs down everyone's throats. And, it's the humanists that are brainwashing all the children with their *evolution* junk."

"Hey, you guys," Terry said, "I know things can be discouraging. But, think about it! This is what *we—the Creation Science Club*—are all about. God has given us a special calling—to go out to Miss Giggles, Mr. Eyebrows, and Mr. Long Locks and give them the *real* facts. Not cramming anything down anyone's throats, not brainwashing anyone. Just giving them the facts, helping them to *discover* the truth for themselves."

"Actually," Cory admitted, "I guess Mr. Long Locks did have the guts to speak up for what he believed. He just didn't have the knowledge to show that what he believes is…well, *believable.*"

"And, Mr. Eyebrows seemed like a thoughtful enough guy," Jack added. "I'll bet if we gave him some *new facts* to think about, he'd be willing to give God the credit for creating the world—instead of Mother Nature."

"Even Miss Giggles had a good point," Bekah put in. "Phil Lovit just scared her off by using that big, 'unarguable' word—*evolution.*"

"Well," Mrs. Carmen said, putting her arm around Billy, "it just goes to show you how much our little town needs a Creation Science Museum like the one Dr. Ted and Dr. Ed are working on."

Billy looked at the news screen, now showing some footage of Big Aug's abandoned car out by Tiller's Hill. "And that brings us right back to an important question: Just who is so dead set against Dr. Ted's Creation Museum that they would hire the Big Auger to break in—not just once, but twice?"

# CHAPTER 7

Arby, one of Billy's big mutts, sat up and sniffed the night air as a shadowy figure darted behind a tree outside the camp. Quietly, he padded over to his sleeping master and began licking Billy's ear.

Billy rolled over and pushed the pooch away, but Arby was right back and licking the other ear. So, Billy sat up and asked in a sleepy voice, "What's goin' on, boy?" Without hesitation, Arby went over to David's sleeping bag and started to whine.

Billy got up and walked over to investigate. The sleeping bag was empty. Billy reached down and gave his dog a pat. "Don't worry, David's just answering nature's call. He'll be back in a minute."

Arby, however, didn't seem to agree. With another whine, he headed up the hill. Billy called him back, and he came, but then turned around and headed toward the woods again. "Okay, okay…" Billy said, with a note of concern in his voice. "You win. I'm coming." And he followed Arby up the hill and into the trees.

Before long, Billy caught sight of the figure of a second dog tracking alongside Arby. It was Rax. Billy had to smile. It was next to impossible to separate those two. Back and forth the dogs zigged and zagged, obviously following a familiar scent.

After a ten-minute hike through the darkness, Billy caught up to the dogs. They were excitedly sniffing at a big jumble of different sized rocks. Billy knew his dogs. He knew how they behaved when they were tracking a rabbit, he knew how they behaved when they were tracking a bobcat, and he knew how they behaved when they smelled a bear.

It was downright obvious that they weren't after any animal they'd dealt with before. So, Billy approached with caution. No cougars had been in these parts for years, but their range was growing. It was best to be careful. He was just about to call the dogs off and head them back down to camp when Arby disappeared through a hole in the rocks. Rax went right behind him.

Billy felt his stomach tighten. If a cougar was in there, both his dogs were in for the fight of their lives. Even a bobcat could cause a lot of damage. He waited, expecting an eruption of hissing and barking. But there was only silence. Crouching down, Billy reached his arm inside the hole and felt around. It was bigger than it looked. Putting his head and shoulders in, he called "Arby! Rax! Come on, you two! Come here!"

After a short wait, he heard the shuffling feet and nervous whines of his dogs. They both quickly took advantage of having him at face level by excitedly licking his face and ears. But, as Billy reached out to grab Rax's collar, Rax backed away and gave a quick bark. Then, he turned around and followed Arby back down the dark tunnel.

What could be going on? The dogs obviously weren't scared of whatever was at the end of the tunnel. And yet, what could it be?

Glad that he'd slept in his jeans, Billy crawled on all fours into the dark passage. Reaching down, he pressed a button to light up the face of his watch—not to see the time, but to see where he was going. It wasn't long before the tunnel opened up into a small cave. Arby and Rax met him again with another round of excited kisses.

Once he had pushed the dogs aside and sat up, Billy held up his watch to look around. Almost immediately, he saw two other people. One was David, looking surprised and guilty. The other was a very large man, with longish hair and a fierce expression on his face—Big Aug Cussler.

Billy didn't hesitate even a second. He grabbed his cell phone. "David! Get over here beside me!" he said in a low, tense voice.

With calm determination, Billy dialed 9-1-1. But, before he could push the send button, David grabbed the phone out of his hand. "No, Billy, wait! Don't call the sheriff. I can explain."

David then flicked on his flashlight, and Billy saw that Big Aug hadn't moved from his crouched position about eight feet away. Billy reached into his pocket and pulled out his pocket knife, but didn't open it. "David," he said firmly, "you may speak once you are behind me. Is that understood?"

"Yes, sir," David said, scooting his way behind Billy until he was mostly in the tunnel, but still facing the small cave. Then, he said, "Listen, Billy! Big Aug is innocent. Honest. Last night, when the police were after him, we…uh…kinda ran into each other and he asked me for help. So, I hid him in this little cave—I just found it the other day. Really, I wanted to tell you, but I wasn't sure how…"

The Big Auger still hadn't moved. Arby went over to him and gave his hand a lick and lay down next to him. This sign of Arby's trust went a long way with Billy, and he visibly relaxed. "Okay," he said, "it seems clear that Augustine, here, isn't a danger to us personally. But, if he's been setting fires for a fee, he has to face the consequences."

"I didn't do it!" Big Aug spoke for the first time. "I was framed."

"Why should we believe you?" Billy asked, keeping David behind him.

"Look, Billy," David said, pointing his flashlight at Big Aug. "Look around his neck. It's his silver bull head necklace. Now, if he broke into Dr. Ted's museum and lost his necklace there by mistake, why would it still be around his neck?"

Billy sighed as he realized that David was right. He scooted farther into the cave, getting a little more comfortable, then asked, "OK, Aug…let's hear your side of the story."

When Big Aug saw Billy put his pocketknife away, he relaxed, too. "Well, y'all know that I've lived a pretty rough life these last several years. Guess I had all kinds of hate and anger just stuck up insida me." Then, rubbing his eyes, he continued, "Anyways, I got tired of it all—tired of the cops and the jail cells. But, tired, too, of bein' mean, and people bein' scared of me and all. So, I went straight. Started to learn to read. Decided to go for my GED." Here he paused. "Miss Abbi sure was good to me." Then, he looked angry. "I wouldn't never do anything to hurt her—so why would I go and try to burn down Dr. Ted's museum? I know they're plannin' on gettin' hitched."

"Well," Billy asked, "do you have any idea why someone might want to frame you?"

Big Aug looked a little uncomfortable, and unsure. But David encouraged him. "It's okay, you can trust Billy."

So, Aug went on. "Couple weeks back, I had two fellas offer me good money to burn down Dr. Ted's museum. I said, *No way!* They offered more money. When I said *No* again, they got mad. I guess they decided they'd find someone else to do their dirty work. But they must've been scared I'd rat on 'em, so they framed me."

Billy was quiet. For a long time, no one said anything. Then, Billy told Big Aug, "Well, Augustine, I believe you. But, I'm not the sheriff. For now, you can stay here in this cave, and our gang will work on finding the real creeps behind all this."

Looking at his watch, Billy told David it was time to get back to camp. But before leaving, he turned to Big Aug and said, "We'll take care of you while you're in this cave. And, unless necessary, we won't tell anyone you're here. However, I'm afraid I can't give you all my trust. If you leave the area, I'll feel it's necessary to call the sheriff and tell him what I know."

The Big Auger nodded his head and answered, "I'll stay right here."

*******

"Meticulous Scientific Study Upholds Evolution," Dr. Nottah read the newspaper headline out loud to his class of honors students. After a pause for effect, he continued with the article's premise. "Dr. Nate Selekson, Professor Donna Taque, and a tireless team of scientists have completed a landmark scientific experiment that gives irrefutable *proof* that one species can evolve into a new species."

Dropping the paper onto his desk, Dr. Nottah turned directly to David and asked, with a note of triumph in his voice, "Well, Mr. Avila, do you care to try and refute the irrefutable."

"Well, sir," David said in a respectful tone, "it seems that many people have the misconception that creationists don't believe in any kind of change at all among animals and plants. But, that's not the way it is." David paused to clarify, "Actually, I guess there are a *very few* that try to say there's no change. But the vast majority of creationists *do* see and acknowledge biological change."

Dr. Nottah nodded. "Well, if you see the change, why do you continue to reject evolution?"

David continued, "You see, creationists claim that change happens *within* a created kind, with mutations and natural selection allowing for adaptation. So, as in the case of the QLU experiment, we creationists already know that a field mouse can change into a desert mouse. However," David emphasized, "creationists do *not* believe that the changes that occur in plants and animals will ever produce a new *kind* of plant or animal. For example, a mouse will never be able to change enough to turn into an elephant."

Several of the students in the room snickered at David's example. But, Dr. Nottah paid no attention to them. He took two steps toward David and asked in a quiet tone, "Are you saying—with certainty—that creationists acknowledge change, and yet reject evolution?"

"Well, yes, sir," David answered calmly. "We believe that mutations and different combinations of the original genetic information within a created kind allow organisms to adapt—over generations—to a new or changing environment."

At this point, Dr. Nottah sat down in the empty desk diagonal from David and responded, "But, isn't that evolution?"

"No," David shook his head. "That's *adaptation*—mutations and natural selection operating on existing biological systems. The information to make a field mouse can be tweaked to make a desert mouse. Scientists can and do observe that kind of change. *Evolution,* by definition, requires a huge amount of new, complex systems added in order for one organism to change into a new, different kind of organism."

"Yes," the teacher agreed with David's statement, but added, "and, when given enough time, such as hundreds of millions of years, these small changes we see today could be as dramatic as changing a mouse into an elephant."

Some of the students giggled again, but David remained serious. "Dr. Nottah," he answered, "just as we saw in your research labs last quarter, any change that anyone has ever observed has been a downhill change—actually breaking down a system that already exists. Mutations and natural selection are not producing the complex new systems required to change a field mouse into an elephant."

Dr. Nottah replied, "We don't really believe that a field mouse changed into an elephant."

"Maybe not," David said, "but you *do* claim that a single-celled organism evolved into humans and all the other variety of life we see today."

"But, given enough time, mutations could…" Dr. Nottah let his words fade.

"The types of changes we observe today," David responded, "are all downhill changes. It's the opposite change your evolution must have in order to turn an amoeba into a man."

"Well, hmmm…" Dr. Nottah paused to digest the significance of David's statement. But, when a few of the students started to whisper, he sat up a little straighter and asked, "Well, what if some other mechanism were responsible for that increase, something scientists are, as of yet, unaware of?"

David shook his head. "Evolutionists boldly claim mutations and natural selection as their driving force—the maker of new information."

"But…but, just suppose…" Dr. Nottah began in a tone already filled with doubt, "that there *is* another driving force at work, a phenomena that we haven't yet discovered. Isn't that possible?"

David met and held Dr. Nottah's gaze. "Sir," he said, "it seems a lot more possible that evolution just isn't true. Have you ever even considered that?" Everyone in the class held their breath, waiting for Dr. Nottah's response.

"Well, no…I haven't," Dr. Nottah said slowly. "To be honest, I've always just accepted that the big bang and evolution were the way that everything was formed out of… well, out of nothing."

"I've heard," David answered, "that the probability of even one—just one—single-celled organism forming out of non-life is about as likely as a tornado going through a junk yard and assembling a 747 jet. Think about it, sir. If that's the probability of the simplest organism forming by evolution, then what are the chances that all the diversity of life we see around us today—and that has existed throughout history—was formed by evolution?"

"Not a chance," the teacher answered, shaking his head. "Not a chance. This is ridiculous! Here I am fumbling for answers…when I've never even considered…" Without finishing his sentence, Dr. Nottah stood up, turned around, and left the room.

*******

Not a sound. Each movement must be silent. One last step gave him a view of the small clearing. There it was! A once in a lifetime chance. The largest rack he'd ever laid eyes on. Slowly…painfully…the hunter took two more steps. He had been tracking this buck for days, and this was the first real visual he had had. After a pause, the hunter began to move—taking a full minute to raise his rifle.

But then, out of the corner of his eye, the man caught a glance of motion to his right. Slow and steady, smooth and fluid, he turned his head toward the movement. *What!* A tiger! A huge Amur tiger was stalking *his* buck! One whiff of that stinkin' cat would send his trophy leaping through the brush—lost, gone, adios! And yet, if he shot at the tiger—bye, bye Mr. Elk!

Moving as quickly and silently as he could, the hunter trained his eyepiece on the buck. He would take out the deer, then turn the rifle on the cat. Maybe this hunt would turn out to be the most super-fantaz-great-spectacular fantasy come true—bagging two large game trophies on the same hunt!

The sweat dripped down his face as he concentrated. He lined up the best shot possible, then moved his finger to the trigger. No worries…like taking candy from a baby.

But, even as he set his finger on the trigger, a silly-faced spider monkey swung down from a branch and started to chatter a loud warning. Both the deer and the tiger snapped their heads toward the monkey, then began looking around for the hidden danger.

"Sockamonaga!" the man thought. "I've been betrayed. Well, it's now or never…" and he took final aim and started to pull his trigger finger back.

"Roooaaarrr!" The very air itself shook. Then suddenly, the hunter felt the rifle being jerked from his hands. Twisting around and falling back against a tree, the man came face to face with a beast. Standing well over six feet on its hind legs, 500 pounds of solid muscle loomed over the paralyzed man. Reaching down, the silverback gorilla grabbed the man up like he was a rag doll. Pulling him to his feet, it put its fangs within inches of the hunter's face. "I win!" it said with a laugh of victory.

The little spider monkey joined the Siberian tiger and the buck as they ran toward the gorilla and the man. "See," the deer told the hunter, "just because you have a gun doesn't mean you'll always win against nature."

"No fair!" the man complained. "It was four against one."

"So?" the tiger growled, "In real life, the hunter often faces even greater odds."

“Okay, okay,” the man said, reaching down to pick up his paint pellet gun. “You guys win this time. But, I still say that God made man with enough smarts to beat out the animals.”

“Maybe so,” the monkey chattered, standing on his back legs and reaching up to remove his *Reality Morphing* glasses. “But, I think God plays fair. While He gave man superior intelligence, so he can make guns and camouflage clothes, He equipped the animals with some awesome instincts that usually leave man crying in their dust.”

The silverback scratched his head and removed his own glasses. “Hey,” Big Aug said to the tiger, “that reminds me of a few questions I had for Billy. D’ya think he could come on up to the cave this afternoon and talk with me for a spell?”

“I’m guessing he’ll be glad to,” David answered. “I’ll ask him and tell you what he says when we bring up your lunch.”

“Thanks,” Big Aug said as he turned to head up the hill. Then he stopped and smiled. “Y’all are great fun. When I was a kid, I thought nothin’ could beat cow tippin’. But, this sure ’nough does.” Then he added with a laugh, “And, it’s even legal. Go figure!”

Darin reached out a hand and Aug met him with a smooth sliding five. Then, the four boys turned and headed down toward the Maple Hill workshop, while the Big Auger climbed up toward the small cave hidden among the rocks.

# CHAPTER 8

## Observable Speciation (Evidence for Evolution?)

by David J. Avila

### Introduction

Evolutionists claim that observable speciation is evidence for evolution. One 'official' definition of evolution is "descent with modification." However, this is a very broad definition that covers *any* biological change we can observe. A brown-eyed couple having a blue-eyed child even fits into this definition. (Is *that* evolution?)

A more accurate understanding of what evolutionists believe is—"All the life forms we see today can trace their origins back to the first single-celled organism." This view of evolution is a belief—an assumption based on existing evidence. It is *not* operational science—it cannot be observed, tested, or repeated.

One line of evidence evolutionists use to support this belief is the concept of speciation. For this report, I will look at evolution's claims regarding speciation and show that the evidence agrees better with what the Bible says—that God created all things according to their kinds.

**Does Speciation Occur?**

A good, simple definition for *species* is "a group of organisms that can interbreed to produce fertile offspring." If one group of organisms cannot produce fertile offspring with another group, the two groups are considered separate species. And, *speciation* is the formation of a *new species*. For example, if a biological change causes a subgroup within a species to no longer breed with the rest of that species, this subgroup would be considered a new, separate species.

The first question to consider is whether or not speciation *really* occurs. All scientists (evolutionists *and* creationists) agree that organisms in nature can adapt to new environments. But, can this adaptation change a sub-group of organisms so much that it is no longer able to produce fertile offspring with its original species? Scientific evidence tells us that the answer is—*yes!* And, observable science shows that this biological change can happen fairly quickly.

One natural example of speciation was observed in the underground train system of London. After migrating into the train system, a new species of underground mosquito formed that can no longer interbreed with the original species.

There has also been laboratory research showing speciation. In some experiments, a subgroup of organisms was selected out of a group based on specific traits, like differences in anatomy, mating behaviors, or habitat preferences. These selected subgroups were bred for several generations, always selecting for certain traits. In this way, scientists 'created' a new species—a subgroup of organisms that did not interbreed with the original group.

So, both natural and laboratory evidence confirm that speciation really can and does occur. *But—is it evolution?*

## Is Speciation Evolution?

Evolutionists claim that observable speciation is evidence for evolution. But, consider the following. If the "first single-celled organism" evolved into the vast variety of life we see today, there would need to be countless new, complex systems added to it. That first cell did not have the information necessary to form fins, scales, wings, legs, arms, etc. So, for speciation to truly support evolution, it would need to be producing new information for those new, complex systems. *But it does not.*

Speciation is caused by mutations and natural selection. Mutations are mistakes made in copying the genetic information of an organism. Mutations *do* cause a change in an organism's genetic make-up. However, those changes do *not* produce *new, complex systems*—they actually break down the systems that already exist. And, natural selection is the 'selecting out' of certain genetic information from within a group of organisms. It *does* result in genetic change within a group. However, this change does *not* produce evolution's *new,* complex systems—it is selecting from what is already there.

So, speciation does *not* produce *new,* complex systems. Instead, it is sorting and changing *existing* information. Therefore, speciation is actually the *opposite* of evolution—existing systems are breaking down. And, this is where the creationists' explanation of speciation comes in.

## Speciation—a Better Explanation

Evolutionists sometimes claim that creationists think organisms do *not* change over time. They imply that creationists reject *any* biological change—even mutations and natural selection. But this is not true. Creationists *know* that living things change. Mutations and natural selection are observable, repeatable science. But creationists *do* reject evolution. And, instead, they offer a much better explanation for the biological change—and speciation—we observe.

Creationists believe that God created all things according to their kinds, just as the Bible says. It's important to understand that the biblical *kind* is a larger group than what is meant by one of today's *species*. Examples of created kinds would include the equine (horse-like) kind, the canine (dog-like) kind, the feline (cat-like) kind, and so on.

It's also important to understand that creationists believe each of the original kinds was created with a *huge* amount of genetic information and potential for change. In this way, God made sure the created kinds had enough variety in their genes so their descendants could adapt to a variety of environments. So, out of the original created kinds, new varieties—and even new species—could form. For example, within the cat kind, we find house cats, tigers, servals, and the African golden cat—different species, but all within the same created cat kind.

Creationists believe that many of the species we see today formed after the Flood of Noah's day. After the worldwide Flood, animals migrated to different areas with various climates and environments. And, because they had a vast variety of genetic information to pull from, they could adapt through mutations and natural selection to survive in their new environments. We believe that many new varieties—and even new species—of animals formed quickly after the Flood.

But again, this is *not* evolution. The changes in the created kinds were *not* the introduction of new, complex systems required by evolution. Rather, the changes were the breaking down of existing systems. Creationists' explanation of observable speciation makes good, scientific sense of the evidence. Evolutionists claim that observable speciation is evidence for evolution—but their belief is *not* supported by the evidence.

**Conclusion**

Evolutionists claim that observable speciation is evidence for evolution. They say speciation proves that all the variety of life forms we see today evolved over billions of years from "the first single-celled organism." But, for evolution to be proven true, there needs to be evidence of genetic change producing new, complex systems. Mutations and natural selection do *not* produce these new systems. Speciation is observable, but it is *not* the result of new, complex systems being produced. In fact, speciation is just the *opposite* of evolution—it is breaking down existing systems. So, speciation is *not* evidence for evolution. Observable speciation does, however, clearly agree with what the Bible says—that God created all things according to their kinds.

*******

Dr. Chance Nottah sat in a quiet cove out on the university grounds with a stack of David's past science reports beside him. Leaning back against a large tree, he sighed. Taking off his glasses and rubbing his eyes, he looked down and thought about his tenure at QLU. He had quite a bit of money saved up; he could just quietly retire. He had always wanted to travel a bit.

Nah, he thought as he looked at the stack of reports. His life had been a quest—a quest for knowledge *and* a quest to pass that knowledge on to others. He could never be happy just walking on some resort beach—knowing that he was hiding a key that could change the way the world viewed… well, viewed *everything*.

Hour after hour, day after day, year after year, he had worked—reading, researching, testing—giving up the best years of his life to advance man's understanding of evolution. He had let his marriage fall apart, lost any real contact with his children, and pulled back from the few Christian friends who would still put up with him. What a betrayal! He had given himself to advance the truth, only to find out he had lost everything for the sake of a lie. Standing up, Dr. Nottah struck the tree with his open hand.

The stinging pain in his hand seemed to make something suddenly clear. No—he had not been so noble as he would like to think. He had not given himself to advance the truth. No—he had given his time, his effort, sacrificed everything to advance *himself*. Innumerable times he had glimpsed the *real* truth. Friends, books, even evolution itself had spoken the truth loud and clear. It was he himself that had covered his ears. He had refused to listen to something that would make him look like a *fool* in the eyes of his peers. He would not be looked down upon. He would not fade away teaching in some unknown, penniless Christian college. Pride—pride had been his master.

Sitting down again, Dr. Nottah opened his laptop and began to type.

**TO: hope@science.qlu.net**
**FROM: chance@science.qlu.net**
**RE: bio questions**

**Dr. Hope,**

**Thank you for your recent reply to my request for a better understanding into some biological questions. Your answers were very informative and helpful.**

**I know Frank has been trying to get me over to your house for the past few years. I can't believe he still talks to me after how I've treated him. I guess that's the sign of a real friend. Anyway, whenever your family is able, I would like to take him up on that invitation. I'm afraid**

**one meeting probably will not suffice. But, it will be a start. We can then go from there.**

**If you'll send me Frank's e-mail address, I'll clue him in on what's going on.**

**Thanks,**

**Chance**

PART 3

# Similar Biological Structures

# CHAPTER 9

The younger half of the recently expanded Creation Science Club sat waiting inside the Maple Hill cabin. David, Jack, and Aaron sat around the computer screen working on an animation program—preparing some video clips for their next science report. Jill, Tasha, and Cory were looking through the latest edition of *Rational Science*. All six looked up expectantly as they heard the sound of an approaching vehicle. But then, they heard shouting. *"Slow down! Pull Over!"* Then came the sound of a sheriff's siren.

The teens hopped up and stood at the cabin windows. Through a cloud of dust, they could just make out Billy's jeep racing up the hill toward them.

"Oh, no!" Cory gasped. "The sheriff must have found out we're helping Big Aug."

David ran toward the cabin's back door. He wasn't sure what he was going to do; he just knew he needed to help Big Aug. But, just as he got to the door, he heard a sudden eruption of laughter. Totally confused, David went back to the front window to see what was going on. It was only a second before he was laughing with the others.

Abel was sitting in the back of the jeep with his hands cupped around his mouth—he was the one making the loud siren sounds. Billy was in the passenger seat with one hand holding his ball cap on his head, while the other hand had a death grip on the jeep door. "I said, *slow down!* The brake! *The brake!* No, the *other* pedal!"

Cory giggled. "I guess Darin started his driving lessons today. I sure hope I wasn't that bad when I first learned."

"Well, it's about time he learned," Jack commented.

Aaron shook his head as the jeep spun to a screeching halt. "I can see why his mom wanted him to wait a couple extra years before he got his license."

David watched as Abel hopped out of the back of the jeep. "I think Abel will be easier to teach. He seems more 'down to earth' than Darin."

As soon as Darin put the jeep in park, he reached out to knuckle-knock his brother who had come around to congratulate him.

"Super-de-cool-fantastico!" Darin laughed. "Am I *bad* or what!" Then he added, "Just think, next time Bekah comes to visit, I'll be able to pick her up from the airport all by myself."

Billy just stayed glued to the passenger seat—in a state of semi-shock.

Once they were all in the cabin, Jack pounced on Darin and dragged him over to the computer for some technical advice. Billy, who was soon back to normal, handed Aaron a large bag from Biggie Burgers. Then, he gave David a stack of books from the library. "Here, why don't you guys take these on up to Tiger Cave for Big Aug?"

"Awesome!" David smiled, and the two of them headed out the back door.

"Hey, Billy," Jill called, "come look at this. We've been looking through the newest *Rational Science*."

"*Rational Science*," Abel said, morphing his voice to a perfect imitation of Nick Foreman (the famous commentator for the hugely successful *World of Rational Science* television program), "bringing you face to face with scientific facts."

Darin looked up from the computer. "Yeah, right, sure!" he rolled his eyes. "It's more like, "*IRrational Science*, bringing you face to face with scientific *fallacy*."

Billy laughed. "That's a good one Darin!" Then he pulled a chair closer to the couch the girls were on. "So, what'd you find?"

Cory held out the magazine. "Look, here's an article about QLU with Dr. Selekson and Professor Taque. Their mouse experiment actually made it into *Rational Science*."

Tasha added, "It's only a page long, pictures included, but look at the title, *Experiment Proves Evolution*."

Abel went back into his Nick Foremen voice. "QLU scientists spend three years and five million dollars to prove the *indisputable* scientific fact of evolution."

Jill smiled, but said in a serious tone, "My dad says that *billions* of dollars are spent each year 'proving' the so-called 'indisputable scientific fact of evolution.' But I say, if evolution is an indisputable scientific fact, why keep spending all that time and money 'proving' it?"

"It's a pretty good sign of some serious insecurity issues if you ask me," Cory said. "It's just ridiculous that the ones who talk the most confidently about evolution are the ones who seem the most insecure."

"Hey," Billy pointed to the magazine cover, "check this out. This is *Red Roma Man*. You know, the supposed 'human ancestor' they found over in France last year."

Darin and Jack ran over to see the picture. "Whoa!" Jack said, "Cool illustration!"

Red Roma Man was seated on a rock at the entrance of a cave. He was carefully creating a work of art on the cave wall. Around his feet were different small 'plates.' Each plate held a different color of 'paint.' On the cave floor, around the plates, were different items used to make the ‘paint’—clay, berries, nuts, mud, blood, flowers, etc.

Red Roma himself was an ape-ish looking man with broad hairy shoulders, long hairy arms, and short hairy legs. And, as one might have guessed, all that hair was decidedly *red.* Now, this description might bring to mind an orangutan. However, the illustration on the cover of *Rational Science* spoke *man* much more than *ape.* For under all that hair, such obvious intelligence shone through that no one would ever guess Red Roma Man to be anything but an ancestor of modern man.

The illustration was titled, *Red Roma Man, France's First Great Artist.*

*******

Sitting up in Tiger Cave, David and Aaron stole a few fries while Big Aug ate his Biggie Burger and Biggie Salad.

“You all have been mighty good to me,” Aug said between bites. “I'd be behind bars for sure if it weren't for you all. And,” he added, “without you bringing me all these books and games, I'd be nuts by now.”

David laughed. “Miss Abigail says that the Lord just wanted to make sure you really learned how to read before He let us clear your name.”

Aug laughed, too, then looked uncertain. “You guys all seem pretty sure that God is watchin' out for me. But, I don't see why He would...” He stopped and sighed. “I ain't nothin' but a no good varmint.”

Aaron sighed too, then answered, “You know, Augustine, we're *all* nothing but ‘no good varmints.’ It says so right in the Bible: ‘For all have sinned and fall short of the glory of God.’ You know, we've all thought and done bad things. We're all sinners.”

"Yeah, I guess so, sorta," Aug said. "But, you all wanna be good. You try to be good. I wanted to be bad. I tried to be bad. You know, 'To hurt and to maim was the Big Auger's favorite game…' Any bad thing you've ever did was nothing compared to what I've done."

"That's probably true," David admitted. "But, look at it this way, God said that every single person must be condemned (for the wages of sin is death) unless we do one of two things. We must either live a 100% perfect life or we must accept Jesus Christ's condemnation and death in our place."

Aaron continued, "No one's perfect—*no one.* So, while it's right to try to live a good life, it can't save you. Salvation comes only through faith in Jesus Christ."

Big Aug looked at the cave floor for a while, then said, "I've heard all that before. And, I really am sorry for the bad things I've done. But…well, it just seems like a cop-out. I mean, here I've lived a worthless waste of a life, but then, when I face real trouble, I go to God and say, 'Hey, I'm sorry. Will ya forgive me?'"

"Yeah," David said, "we all kinda feel like that. But, if you really are sorry, God really forgives you. It's that simple."

Aaron spoke up, "There's a story in the Bible that explains it really well. It's like this... There were these two bad men. Both of them were bad—really bad. They were so bad that they were going to be put to death. They were the men who were crucified on the right and left of Jesus. One of them knew that he was bad, and he knew that Jesus claimed to be able to 'save' people. But, he decided to reject Jesus and mocked Him.

"But the other guy was different. He was just as bad as the first guy, maybe even worse. But he decided to accept Jesus' offer of salvation. So, he looked at Jesus and asked Him to remember him when Jesus entered His kingdom."

"And," David finished, "Jesus told him, 'I tell you the truth, you will be with me in paradise.' It was that simple."

Big Aug nodded, but didn't say anything.

# CHAPTER 10

David smiled as he filed off the school bus with the other eighth grade honors science students and their tutors. Today's field trip promised to be interesting. Looking around, David saw Billy at the front of the line.

Billy and Dr. Nottah were discussing their expectations concerning today's tour. Dr. Nottah told Billy, "I planned this trip to Brignut's Science Center as soon as I was stuck with the DMS principal's job. I have a friend who does the tours here." He paused to chuckle. "Boy, is Justin going to be surprised by my recent, uh…re-evaluation of the theory of evolution."

Billy smiled. "Darin and Abel know Mr. Faith pretty well. They used to come here with their dad all the time. Before Mr. Tadue died, their family lived just about five miles from here. And, as you probably know, Mr. Faith has a son with high-functioning autism, so he was always very good and patient with the T-twins."

Dr. Chance paused, then asked in a quiet tone, "So, Abel and Darin have high-functioning autism?"

"Actually, they have Asperger Syndrome. Doctors consider it to be in the same 'spectrum' as autism, but there are still a lot of differences between the two."

"Oh! There's a guy that works in the QLU research lab that calls himself an *Aspie*. He's real smart but doesn't have a clue about how to relate to people about anything outside of the lab."

Billy nodded. "Well, those two traits are the primary definition of AS—above average intelligence and an inborn lack of social skills."

Dr. Chance looked back at Darin and Abel. "I don't know…those two are *different*, but they're well dressed and have good manners and all."

Billy paused to look at his two young friends. "Actually, it's been unconditional love and acceptance, plus a lot of consistent, patient instruction, that has taught the T-twins how to interact so well with others."

Dr. Chance had to chuckle as he watched Abel throw back his head and laugh at something Darin had said. "Well, I have to admit, their obvious love for life and fun is pretty contagious."

Billy smiled. "You don't know the half of it."

In the back of the line, Abel and Darin were teasing one of the other tutors. "Hey, Mrs. Mary," Darin said with a disarming smile, "I've heard some mouth-watering rumors about your apple strudel, double-caramel deluxe pie."

Now, Mrs. Mary had made quite an effort over the last several months *not* to like David and his creationist buddies. But, she couldn't help but soften at this compliment to her baking. "And," she said in response, "I've heard that you have a 'totally awesome' Computer Tutor that my daughter is dying to get her hands on."

Abel took advantage of the small crack in her shell. "So, it's your deluxe pie against Darin's Computer Tutor. Hmmm…we've got the stakes…that means, all we need now is a bet."

As the group walked into the front hall of the elaborate building, Mrs. Mary was feeling pretty confident. "Okay," she said, "I'll bet Mr. Faith's tour will make your creationist ideas look—outright silly. Now, what do you think of that?"

Darin raised one eyebrow and replied, "Acceptable. Now, for my side. I'll bet that Mr. Faith gets so flustered during the question/answer session at the end of the tour that he stomps his right foot twice, pulls on his left ear three times, and then stomps his left foot once before he calls an early end to the session because he can't adequately answer our group's questions."

Mrs. Mary couldn't help but laugh as she reached out to shake Darin's extended hand. "It's a deal," she said. "But, you should realize, young man, that the more detail in the bet, the harder it is to win."

Darin just smiled. "Madam, I am not at all worried." Then they all headed into the Center's private theater.

*******

During the tour's lunch break, Jack, David, and Aaron shared a small table in the cafeteria. "Blah, blah, blah," Jack said. "Mr. Faith is just like my uncle. It seems like evolutionists always have plenty to say about anything and everything. They just talk and talk and talk with all their fancy words, but always get irritated if you question what they're saying."

"Well," David smirked, "you shouldn't have tried to ask anything. Remember, he made it clear at the beginning that all questions needed to be held until the end of the tour."

"Yeah," Aaron added, "I guess he didn't want anyone ruining his memorized spiel by questioning its accuracy right from the start."

*******

At the end of the tour, Mr. Faith called the group back into the theater for a time of questions. As they entered, Darin and Abel overheard Mrs. Mary telling her daughter, Janie, that Darin was going to let her use his Computer Tutor for her next science report.

"Hmmm!" Darin snorted. "I guess she thinks she's won. But, the game isn't over yet."

Abel nodded. Then, rubbing his hands together, he said, "Actually, the game is just about to begin."

In the theater, Mr. Justin Faith stood up front and said that he was ready to entertain some questions, but stipulated that the questions must be only of a scientific nature and must come only from information covered during the tour.

Jack had his hand up first. "Yes, young man," Mr. Faith said with a smile that was too big. "You are the one who was so eager to speak earlier. Now, what is it you wish to ask?"

"Well, sir," Jack said, "when we were viewing the Common Biological Structures display, you said that the similarities between apes and humans are solid scientific evidence that apes and humans evolved from a common ancestor."

"Yes, yes," Mr. Faith nodded confidently.

"So, you're saying that because apes have five fingers just like we do, that's evidence that we evolved from the same five-fingered ancestor."

"Yes, yes. It does seem quite obvious, now, doesn't it?" Justin Faith said, ready to move on to the next question.

"But, but," Jack waved his hand to continue, "what about the fact that frogs have five fingers just like we do. Is that evidence that we evolved from a common five-fingered ancestor? I mean, from what I understand, human fingers and frog fingers form in very different ways."

The tour guide stopped smiling for a minute and looked at Dr. Nottah, who 'just happened' to be looking away at the moment.

"Well, this would be an example of what we call *convergent evolution*—that is, evolution along different lines of descent, which means not from a common ancestor." Without pausing to let Jack speak, Mr. Faith continued, "Does anyone *else* have a question for me?"

A girl in the back raised her hand. "Sir, we learned about convergent evolution in science class using the example of the squid eye and the human eye."

"Yes, yes, scientists tell us that the squid eye and the human eye appear similar in some ways but evolved separately, along two separate lines of descent, not from a common ancestor."

"So," the girl continued in a confused tone, "that would mean that these common biological structures *aren't* evidence of evolution from a common ancestor?"

Justin Faith again looked toward Dr. Nottah, who this time was decidedly looking at the notes on his lap. Looking back at the girl, Mr. Faith stomped his right foot twice. Abel smiled and leaned over to whisper something to Mrs. Mary. She looked surprised, but not worried.

"Correct, not in this case," Mr. Faith answered the girl. "But, in some cases, some similar biological structures are evidence of evolution from a common ancestor. In some cases, they are not."

Jill raised her hand. "Mr. Faith, could you please clarify? I mean, before lunch, you said that common biological structures are strong evidence for evolution from a common ancestor. But now you're saying that common biological structures might not be evidence for evolution from a common ancestor. Is that right?"

"Yes, yes. I mean, no," Mr. Faith said in a frustrated tone. "Before lunch, I was speaking about, um, well, regular evolution. Just now, we were speaking about convergent evolution. But, the difference between the two *isn't* so important. What *is* important is that they both clearly support the theory of evolution."

"But, I must be missing something," Jill said meekly. "To say that similar traits from a common ancestor and similar traits from different ancestors *both* support the theory of evolution doesn't seem to make sense."

"It makes perfect sense," Mr. Faith said, again trying (and failing) to catch Dr. Nottah's eye. "It makes perfect sense because we know the lines of descent that we are working with. So, we know if the evidence fits evolution from a common ancestor, or if it better fits evolution from different ancestors."

"So, how do you know the lines of descent?" a boy asked.

"From the evidence of common biological structures!" Mr. Faith stated, reaching up to pull on his left ear, one... two...three times. Again, Abel leaned toward Mrs. Mary. She nodded and started to look worried.

"And how do you know if the evidence fits a common ancestor or convergent evolution?" Aaron asked.

"From the lines of descent!" Mr. Faith nearly shouted.

Here, Dr. Nottah finally looked up. "But, Justin," he said calmly, "that is clearly circular reasoning. It cannot be used to prove anything. It just shows that a conclusion has already been predetermined no matter what the evidence shows."

Justin Faith glared at Dr. Nottah. He started to answer, then stopped. He opened his mouth again...but stopped. Finally, he shook his head and said, "We are just going around in circles here." Then, realizing what he had just said, he stomped his left foot and declared, "That is the end of our question/answer session!" And he quickly left the theater by the back exit.

As everyone got up out of their seats, Jack turned to David and said smugly, "I guess our tour guide hasn't been looking at the real evidence, but has been accepting the 'truth' of evolution *just in faith.*"

"*Just in faith...Justin Faith...*Good one, man!" David laughed. "I guess, when it comes down to it, evolutionists have all predetermined the conclusion that evolution is a fact. It's sorta like we put our faith in the truth of God's Word. The problem is, the evidence supports our faith in God's Word, but stands against their faith in evolution."

As everyone filed out of the theater, Darin, Abel, and Mrs. Mary remained in their seats. Mrs. Mary sat like one stunned. Finally, she turned to Darin. "I have spent this entire year with my fingers in my ears. I have refused to listen to a thing you creationists have said. Now, the first time I take my fingers out of my ears, I realize that I have been hard-headedly refusing to even consider anything but what I wanted to believe—even against the evidence."

Abel patted Mrs. Mary on the shoulder. "Don't feel too bad. At least now, you're a mile ahead of the rest—they've still got their fingers in their ears."

As the three stood up to join the others, Mrs. Mary told Darin, "I'll have your deluxe pie ready early next week."

Darin rubbed his hands together in delighted anticipation, then showed his good sportsmanship by saying, "And you can tell Janie that she can use my Computer Tutor for her next report."

Mrs. Mary laughed. "Well, actually, I guess I already did."

*******

Slithering out of the briny waters, the giant sea serpent headed toward the work shed. He needed to use the restroom. But as soon as he flipped on the work shed light, he knew something was terribly wrong. David turned and ran back toward the pond. "Billy! Darin! Come quick! Someone's ruined all the animatronics in the work shed!"

Everyone stood dripping inside the work shed doorway. What they saw was pretty sobering. Two nearly complete animatronic displays for Dr. Ted's museum lay demolished on the floor. The vandals had done a thorough job. It looked doubtful that anything could be salvaged. Darin and Abel started to cry. And Billy headed up to the house to call the sheriff.

*******

"Looks like whoever's out to shut down Dr. Ted's Creation Museum just went too far in the public's eye," Billy said as he sat down with the rest of the gang at Favorite Flavors.

"Why do you say that?" Tasha asked as she dug into her Banana Blitz Sundae.

"Well, I just got off the phone with Dr. Ed. He said that since the paper wrote about Darin and Abel's displays being destroyed last week, they've received ten times more in donations in the past five days than they'd received in the past five months."

"Totally tubularly spectacular!" Darin said with his mouth full of his Peanut Butter Bonanza Sundae.

Billy smiled, but then shook his head. "The only thing that really worries me is that everyone—including Sheriff Murphy—is calling Big Aug the number one suspect. And I can't stand up for him without the risk of exposing him before we have proof of his innocence."

"Anybody have any ideas, yet, on who those two men were who tried to hire Augustine to break into the museum in the first place?" David asked.

"Not really," Billy sighed. "Dr. Ted and Dr. Ed are both so busy with museum stuff that they hardly have time to eat or sleep. The only clues we have to go on are what Big Aug told us—they talked like 'stuck-up, educated city folks.'

They drove a fancy Lexus. They seemed 'over the hill.' And, he heard one of them mention a woman's name—Anita."

* * * * * * *

David was scarfing down a giant pile of chicken and rice when Cory stood up with a gasp, dumping Lumpy, her cat, right off her lap. "What's the matter?" David asked.

"Look at this!" Cory said in a shaky voice. "Here, on the front page, near the bottom."

David wiped his mouth and took the paper to read, "*Local Creation Museum Scams for Donations*." David pushed himself back from the table in disbelief, but continued to read. "A reliable source claims to have proof that Dr. Theodore Veritas and Dr. Edward Lution are themselves behind the break-ins at Dr. Veritas's museum. The anonymous source says that the two separate break-ins on the museum itself and the vandalism at a private workshop were purposely staged to draw sympathy and donations from locals." David stood up and walked toward the phone as he continued reading. "When asked if the source believed Big Aug Cussler had been involved, he said, 'I don't know the answer to that. However, it is just as likely as not that Veritas and Lution framed the Big Auger for their own gain.'"

As David reached for the phone, it rang. It was Aaron on his cell phone, and he sounded really panicked. "David! Man! I was bringing lunch up to Big Aug. But, he's gone. I mean, really gone. I found today's paper with his breakfast stuff. And David, he left his bull's head necklace behind on the lamp we hung up for him in Tiger Cave."

David leaned against the wall. "What are you sayin'? Why would he leave his necklace?"

"Look, man," Aaron said in a worried voice, "I don't know for sure. But, it looks like maybe Aug's decided to turn himself in to Sheriff Murphy."

Cory had picked up the other line and interrupted, "Does Billy know? Have you talked to Billy?"

"Yeah, Billy was here," Aaron answered. "He's already on his way to Sheriff Murphy's office. And he sent the T-twins running through the back-woods short cut to town. They're hoping to meet up with Aug before anyone sees him."

"Well," David asked, "is there anything we can do? Did Billy say there was anything we could do to help?"

"Get up here, man!" Aaron was out of breath, like he was running. "Billy wants someone to stay at the Maple Hill cabin, and someone else at Tiger Cave—just in case Augustine comes back."

"We'll be there!" David said and hung up the phone. Cory grabbed her purse and ran to tell their mom what was going on. Mrs. Avila hurried outside with Cory and David to drive them up to Maple Hill.

# CHAPTER 11

Everyone sat together around a large table in Dr. Ted's museum. Billy had called an emergency meeting. Big Aug had turned himself in. He had not actually confessed to the crimes, but he had not clearly claimed his innocence either. Instead, he had gone to the sheriff (without his bull-head necklace) and told him that it was two rich, old men who had offered him money to vandalize the museum. He'd made it clear to the sheriff, and to the press, that neither Dr. Ted nor Dr. Ed had anything to do with the vandalism. So, for now, the Big Auger was behind bars.

Miss Abbi sat next to Dr. Ted, wiping the tears from her eyes. "I can't believe Augustine sacrificed himself, just to save the museum's reputation."

"It sure shows how much he appreciates our friendship and help," Mrs. Carmen responded. "I only wish he would've talked with us first. Certainly, we could have come up with a better way."

Cory looked really worried. "That necklace was his best proof that he was framed. Why did he leave it behind?"

Dr. Ed spoke up, "I'm guessing he knows the missing necklace will make a lot of people assume he's guilty. I think he wants people to blame *him* rather than Dr. Ted and me."

Tasha sighed. "I *hate* to think of him rotting away in that jail."

"He's not rotting away," Billy smiled. "He'll be more comfortable in jail than he was in Tiger Cave. And Sheriff Murphy is taking everything we told him into consideration. He seems fairly convinced that Big Aug isn't the vandal after all." Billy sighed. "It's really just Augustine's own reputation that's keeping him in jail until the real culprits can be found."

"Then, let's find them!" Aaron slapped his leg impatiently.

"But how?" Cory asked in an exasperated tone.

"Let's find out the name behind that 'reliable source'—the creep who gave the phony tip to the paper," Aaron answered.

"Great idea!" David said jumping up. "You know, my mom has a friend who works at the paper. Maybe she could find something out for us."

"It's a start," Dr. Ted said, nodding his head.

Dr. Chance looked thoughtful, then said, "And I think I'll just go ahead and visit an 'over the hill' ex-friend of mine from the QLU Board. If I remember right, he just bought a fancy new Lexus last year."

"And, here's another clue," Carmen added. "Sheriff Murphy said that Tiny and Bob—two local trouble-makers—have been showing off a couple of mighty nice motorcycles around town. Sheriff says the bikes are legal, paid for in full—with cash. Bob and Tiny told him that they'd been saving a long time to get the bikes. But the sheriff says that's about as likely as it snowing in the Sahara." Then she looked over at Darin and Abel. "I'll bet we could use a couple of your inventions to check up on those two."

Darin was on his feet in an instant. "Oh, oh, I know! Give me 48 hours and some *Cola Super Max,* and I'll make a *Panoramic Global Field Module* that can give us 24/7 visual access to anywhere and everywhere they go on those new bikes of theirs."

Aaron leaned forward. "Dude, we don't have 48 hours—*Cola Super Max* or no *Cola Super Max*."

Darin looked crest-fallen until Abel spoke up. "We could just use our *Ultimate Undetectable Location Monitoring* devices."

"That's it!" Darin was all smiles again.

"Uhhh…translation, please," Tasha requested.

Billy laughed. "I think they're referring to a tracking bug."

"That's exactly right," Darin beamed. "Now, all we have to do is figure out how to get those bugs onto Bob and Tiny's motorcycles."

*******

Lowering himself onto his belly, David worked his way through the tall grasses around the creek. It took a while, but he finally reached the edge of a small clearing. Now, he was just a few feet away from his goal—a chrome-accented black Harley motorcycle.

David focused his eyes on the opposite side of the clearing. And, after a short wait, he saw Cory's face appear. Her goal was the classic blue Harley next to the one David was targeting. Once Cory gave the *thumbs-up*, David pressed two buttons on his *Muf-ToW* band (*multi-functional telecom wristband*). Then, Cory and David hunkered down and waited for the signal to move ahead.

Just 50 feet away, two scroungy-lookin' men sat on the bank of the creek.

The shorter of the two smacked at his neck and then slapped at his arm. "Hey, Bob, I thought ya said the cigarette smoke would keep these skeeters off me. Man, I got three butts goin' over here, and I still keep gettin' bit."

Bob, a big beefy guy, rolled his eyes and reeled in his fishing line. "Man, Tiny, this ain't no better than the slammer.

I'm gonna die if we don't get outta here soon so we can have some fun."

Tiny scoffed at his friend. "Get a grip." After casting out his own line, he emphasized, "We was told to lay low and 'be good' until the next hit."

Bob growled as he swatted at a bite on his shoulder. "But, I ain't used to havin' any boss to answer to. I liked it better when we did what we wanted, when we wanted."

"I didn't hear you complainin' none about a boss when you was showin' off your new ride to Candy down at the Hog's Den."

Bob smiled and laid down his pole to steal a glance at his new bike. But, as he stood up, he felt the sting of several mosquitoes on his back. "Man," Bob grumbled as he waved his arms all around. "Let's get outta here. I'm gettin' eaten alive!"

*Bam!* Just then, Tiny's fishing pole bent down under the weight of a big catch. "Hey, Bob!" Tiny yelled. "Check this out. It must be a monster!"

As Bob turned to see what was happening with Tiny, his own fishing pole started to bend and twist. He grabbed it up before it was pulled into the water. "Hey, I got one too. Mine's a giant. I think it's gonna break my line!"

While Bob and Tiny were struggling with their poles, David and Cory, now together, were crawling back through the tall grass and toward the road—mission accomplished.

Across the creek, Aaron and Tasha held their 'mosquito' pellet guns in their teeth as they scrambled down out of their ambush trees and then off into the woods.

Billy was watching from a distance. And, as soon as he saw all four kids safely away, he pushed a button on his own Muf-ToW. Almost immediately, Tiny fell back onto the bank with a snapped line. Jumping over to Bob's pole, Tiny pulled with him, but then, that line snapped, too.

"Man, what d'ya think them was?" Bob panted. "I ain't never felt a tug like that before."

Tiny looked thoughtful as he tied a new hook on his line. "Well, I've heard that them big carp sometimes swim in pairs…must be what we had."

A ways upstream, Abel and Darin swam toward the reeds where they could climb out—without being seen—to join the others.

Back by the bank, Bob looked all around and then sat down with a smile. "Anyhows, it seems like we scared all them pesky skeeters away."

Once the CSC gang was a good distance up the road, Tasha poked Aaron in the ribs. "You owe me two bucks—I hit Bob way more than you got Tiny."

Aaron shook his head. "No way, Sis! The bet's off. Your target was twice as big as mine."

Billy laughed. "You all did fantastic. Both bikes are now equipped with the T-twins' tracking devices. So, let's get to town and give their signals to Sheriff Murphy."

Darin turned around and started walking backward. "Um, Billy…unless you want a mutiny on your hands, I think you'd better feed this here carp and his brother *before* we go and see the sheriff."

"Hey!" Aaron said. "Don't forget the mosquitoes. We need to eat, too."

Billy looked at David and Cory. "So, we've got two carp and two skeeters. What about you guys—what are you?"

David answered in a very serious tone, "We're *hungry!*"

Everyone laughed and piled into the van.

*******

Sitting at the dinner table, Jack and Jill knew their uncle had something on his mind. But they weren't sure what. Once or twice, they tried to start a conversation with him, but he didn't really seem interested in talking. It was rather awkward.

Finally, Uncle Carl put down his fork and cleared his throat. Mrs. Hill looked up at her brother. "Aren't you hungry, Carl? You usually love my chicken and dumplings."

"The food's fine, Linda. I've just got something weighing on my mind." Uncle Carl looked a bit hesitant, but then continued. "The fact of the matter is, I've got a problem with some of the things going on at QLU. At first, I just thought that Jack and Jill, with all their talk, had made me unduly suspicious. But, the more I see and hear, the more I'm starting to really wonder."

Jill leaned forward eagerly. "Do you mean you've seen something that might help prove Big Aug is innocent?"

Uncle Carl sighed and pushed himself back from the table. "I don't know, maybe. Turns out that QLU has been quietly—very quietly—working on a levy for next year's tax ballot. I guess it would give QLU fifty million dollars over the next five years."

*"Fifty million dollars!"* Mr. Hill gasped. "No way is our small-town county gonna vote that through!"

"Well, no...not if it's presented for what it really is," Uncle Carl agreed. "I've heard some of the higher ups talking here and there. I guess they've got it pretty well planned. It will come through sounding like a major educational benefit for the students of all ages in our area—bringing our 'backwoods' community into the 21st century and all that. But, in reality, 75% of the money will simply go to wherever the QLU Board 'deems best.'"

"That's a lot of money to be floating around in the nebulous realm of 'wherever the QLU Board deems best,'" Jack said with his eyes wide open.

"You know, Carl," Mr. Hill said, "the folks that sign your paycheck aren't going to like it if you start talking around town about this."

"But, Uncle Carl," Jill interrupted, "you said that you knew something that might help to prove Big Aug's innocence."

Uncle Carl nodded. "Well, you guys know what a stubborn man I can be. I can't help it. I'm a scientist. *Facts*—that's what's important. You twins have been very, uh, let's say *persistent* in presenting the many facts in favor of biblical creation. I'll have to say, it's gotten me thinking."

Jill wanted to scream, but instead she calmly asked, "So, how does all this help Big Aug?"

"Well, I guess I'm not the only one in this area that's starting to take a second look at the creation/evolution debate. So, now, consider this: in order for this tax levy to go through, folks around here need to 'believe in' what QLU is doing. They need to think QLU is our future. So, now, here's where the trouble comes in. If folks start thinking about creation science, they're gonna start having trouble with QLU's obvious evolutionary bias."

"Ahhh…" Mr. Hill said, "I think I see what you're saying. The big wigs at QLU are starting to get nervous with all this creation stuff catching on. The more people start believing the Bible's explanation of creation as scientifically possible (even probable), the less they'll be into supporting QLU as their educational future."

"And," Jack concluded, "the less likely they'll be to vote for giving QLU fifty million in tax dollars. So, it would make perfect sense for the big wigs to want to stop our creation movement."

Uncle Carl nodded again. "I heard that Dr. Anita Moore-Power—the university president—nearly threw poor Dr. Nottah out of the board meeting when he said that 'creationism deserved a closer look.'"

"Dr. Moore-Power…" Mrs. Hill wrinkled her nose. "What a greedy sounding name."

Uncle Carl laughed. "She was married when well into her 40s. So, she decided just to attach her husband's last name onto her own maiden name. Anyway, you can imagine all the whispered puns going around the university."

Jill suddenly stood up. "Wait a minute! Anita! Did you say that the president of QLU is named Anita?"

"Yes." Uncle Carl looked puzzled at Jill's excitement.

Now Jack was standing, too. "You aren't gonna believe this, but Big Aug said that the two guys who tried to hire him to do their dirty work mentioned a woman's name—Anita."

# CHAPTER 12

## Similar Biological Structures (From a Common Ancestor?)

by David J. Avila

### Introduction

When we look around us, we observe that many living organisms have similar biological structures—such as lungs, fingers, or eyes. In fact, it has been found that, even on the smallest level, all organisms share a common 'building block'—DNA. It is the goal of a scientist to explore, understand, and explain these similarities.

Evolution claims that similar biological structures are solid evidence that all life on earth evolved from a common ancestor. Creation claims that similar biological structures are evidence that all life on earth was designed by a common Creator.

For this report, I will consider evolution's view of biological structures more closely. Then, I will explain how new scientific discoveries show that the evidence makes better sense when interpreted according to what the Bible says—that all living things were designed and made by a common Creator—God.

**Similar Structures—Proof of a Common Ancestor?**

Evolutionists claim that similar biological structures point to a common ancestor from the distant past. Consider lungs. Lungs are found in a variety of living organisms—frogs, lizards, pigs, humans. Evolution says this similar structure (lungs) proves that these organisms evolved from a common ancestor that also had lungs. But, this 'supposed' ancestor's evolutionary changes cannot be observed or tested today. So, this is not operational science—it's just a belief. Therefore, scientists must look closely at the available evidence to make sure it really does support their belief.

Let's look at the similar structure of five fingers on frogs and five fingers on humans. Evolutionists say this similar feature makes it obvious that frogs and humans share a common ancestor. However, recently, scientists have discovered that the fingers on frogs and the fingers on humans form in very different ways. On a frog, the fingers grow outwardly from separate buds. But on a human, a single ridge forms at the end of the limb, then the material between the fingers dissolves away, leaving the fingers. For the common ancestor argument to be true, the fingers of frogs and humans should form in the same way. So, this evidence conflicts with evolution's belief that similar structures point to a common ancestor.

Now, let's look at the similar structure of the squid eye and the human eye. You would think that evolutionists would claim that this similar structure points to a common ancestor, just as with fingers. However, evolutionists believe that squids and humans evolved along separate lines of descent. For this reason, they have decided that these similar structures do *not* point to a common ancestor. Instead, they say that these similar structures (eyes) evolved separately and are similar only by random chance (Wow, they should definitely buy some lottery tickets).

So, evolutionists say that the similar structures (squid eyes and human eyes) *do not* point to a common ancestor, yet, at the same time, they say that the similar structures (frog fingers and human fingers) *do* point to a common ancestor. But this doesn't make sense! How can they claim that some similar structures *do* point to a common ancestor and that other similar structures *do not* point to a common ancestor, and yet claim that they both still support evolution? They're saying that *opposite* conclusions *both* support their belief in evolution. This use of the evidence just doesn't seem logical!

**Similar Structures—Proof of a Common Creator**

Creationists claim that similar structures, like lungs or fingers or eyes, point to a common Creator. This belief contradicts evolution's claim that 'science *must* have a natural explanation.' It is scientific, of course, to conclude that something is the result of a natural cause. For example, a scientist examining a smooth rock found down by a stream that happens to look like a bird would most likely conclude that it was the work of random erosion.

But, it is just as scientific to conclude that something is the work of a creator. For example, a scientist examining a flint stone chipped into the shape of an arrowhead would most likely conclude that it was the work of a creator. So, it is a scientific process to decide what is the result of nature and what is the work of a creator.

But, evolutionists have completely eliminated the choice that something might be the work of a creator. What they are doing is the same as someone claiming that all rocks—arrowheads, bricks, millstones, or even the Parthenon—could only have been formed by natural causes. This is crazy—but this is what evolutionists are saying by claiming that all the magnificent life around us can only have a natural cause.

It is more rational—and scientific—to keep a creator as a possible cause.

Now, back to the evidence of similar biological structures and the belief in a Creator. Creationists believe that the Master Designer used similar structures on a variety of organisms. Just as a carpenter can put a door on a cupboard, a door on his house, and a door on his barn—so the Creator can put lungs in frogs and humans, and similar eyes in humans and squids.

Creation (just like evolution) is historical science—it cannot be observed or tested today. However, in the case of fingers on frogs and humans, and the similar eye of squids and humans, the belief in a common Creator makes better scientific sense than evolution's belief in a common ancestor.

**DNA—Proof of a Common Ancestor?**

All living organisms contain DNA. Evolution claims this as proof that all living things come from a common ancestor—the first single-celled organism. And, they say that the amount of similarity between the DNA of two different organisms shows how closely they are related on the evolutionary tree. For example, the DNA of a banana is about 50% 'similar' to that of a human. However, the DNA of a chimp is around 95% 'similar' to that of a human. Therefore, evolutionists say that chimps are closer to humans on the evolutionary tree than bananas are.

Now, who would argue with that? Well, creationists do. Why? It's because creationists do not believe that there is an evolutionary tree. Instead, creationists say that these similarities and differences are the work of a common Creator.

Consider the creations of an architect. One architect can design three different buildings—a 30-story office building to work in, a two-story hotel to vacation in, and a log cabin to get away from it all. Obviously, the materials used to build the office building and the hotel would be more similar to each other than they would be to the log cabin. But, still, many of the basic building materials for all three structures would be the same—wood, metal, and glass.

Creationists believe that God chose to use DNA as the basic building block for all living things. Therefore, it makes sense that the more similar living things are, the more similar their DNA would be. So, of course, the DNA of any mammal should be more similar to the DNA of a human than to the DNA of a plant. In the same way, the DNA of a social group of omnivorous apes (chimps) should be more similar to humans than the DNA of a banana. Creationists believe these similarities and differences point to a common Creator, just like the three different buildings all point to a common architect.

**Conclusion**

Many living organisms have similar structures—such as lungs, fingers, eyes, and even DNA. Evolution claims that these similar biological structures are evidence that all life on earth evolved from a common ancestor. Creation claims that similar biological structures are evidence that all life on earth was designed by a common Creator. Both ideas are only beliefs—neither evolution nor creation can be observed or tested. Therefore, only careful consideration of the evidence can show which belief makes better scientific sense. And, in the cases of fingers and eyes, the evidence shows it is more scientific to conclude that all living things were designed and made by a common Creator—God.

*******

Big Aug sat down on the cot in his small cell and leaned against the wall. In one hand, he held the Bible Billy had brought him from Tiger Cave. In the other, he held a stack of four chocolate-chip cookies Mrs. Carmen had baked for him. Each hand held something that had turned Aug's old view of life upside-down—in one hand, the story of *God's* love for him, in the other, the story of *people's* love for him. In a way, both seemed equally important to Augustine. However, something told him that Billy and the gang's kindness to him was really just a personification of God's love for him.

Tony Cussler had been Aug's father—a huge man, with a kind heart. However, he hadn't done well in school and had dropped out the day he turned 16. He had gone to work and had made good money as a logger. Then, at 18, Tony Cussler had met Cindy Schmidt, Aug's mother. She had been only 15 at the time. Her father was an alcoholic, and her mother could barely feed and clothe their five children. Tony and Cindy were married the day after she turned 16. Augustine became a part of their happy home a little over a year later.

But then, tragedy had struck. Tony, Aug's dad, had been killed in a logging accident. And so, Cindy was left a widow with a baby before her 18th birthday. Circumstances forced her to move back in with her parents. Life for Augustine became a blur of sharp words and hard knocks. By ten years old, Aug had already been brought home by the sheriff twice. At 13, he was sent to reform school for a year. And the day he had turned 16, he left school for good. He had been in and out of trouble with the law ever since.

Very early on, Aug had told himself that he didn't need anyone. But, his heart told him differently. Each time he was arrested, he couldn't help but wonder if maybe his mom would come and get him out of jail, or at least come to visit him. But she never did. How he longed for a mother's love.

Then, one day, he had wandered into the town's new library. He'd always been fascinated with wildlife, so he started looking around for some animal picture books. He didn't have much luck until the sweetest lady he had ever met came to his aid. That lady was Abigail Informed. For no reason he could discern, she had taken him under her wing and…well, *loved* him.

That day had changed his view of life. Over the next few weeks, he began meeting with Miss Abbi for reading lessons. He determined that he was going to straighten out his life and be the kind of a man his father had been. But then, there had been the fire at Dr. Ted's museum. All the clues had pointed to him. And now, here he was, in jail—again.

As Augustine was thinking through his past, he was filled with all sorts of thoughts and feelings—regret, sorrow, anger, hatred…and hope. As he looked up and out his small cell window, the Lord spoke to his heart. And Augustine suddenly understood. He had been in a sort of jail his entire life. He had been trapped, held captive by sin—both his own sin and the sin of others. He could turn his life around and be 'good,' but he still wouldn't be free. Still, the sin of his own heart, and the sins of others, would hold him back and keep him from being the man he was created to be. Finally, what Billy, David, and the others had been telling him made sense. Only Jesus Christ could truly set him free.

Switching off the light, the Big Auger knelt beside his cot with the moonlight shining down through his cell window. Then, opening his Bible to John 3:16, he bowed his head and prayed.

PART 4

# Bad Design

# CHAPTER 13

Sheriff Shane Murphy looked at Big Aug's empty cell, then turned back to his desk. He had work to do, and people to call. If everything was going to work out exactly as planned, time was of the essence.

On the evening news, Jeane Jennings reported, "Sheriff Murphy says that it appears Big Aug Cussler escaped his low-security cell through one of the windows. He has stated that it looks like it was an inside job. At this point, there are no clues. The sheriff, however, feels certain that the Big Auger is already on his way out of the state.

The screen showed a picture of an empty jail cell and a pretty scary mug shot of Big Aug. Then, Jeane Jennings concluded, "Well, with Big Aug's long record of trouble, Greenville is ready to see the last of him. Hopefully, in another state, he can start a new, crime-free life."

*******

David and Aaron stopped short as they entered their science classroom, causing a minor traffic jam of students behind them. Aaron turned to Jill and said, "Looks like the 'big wigs' have x-ed Dr. Nottah, and put in Mr. Faith, the tour guide from Brignut's Science Center."

The usually talkative pupils filed silently into the room and nervously took their seats. Mr. Justin Faith looked just as nervous as his students. After pulling at his ear a few times, he cleared his throat and began. "Good afternoon, class. I am Mr. Faith. I believe you all remember me from your recent visit to Brignut's Science Center. The school board has asked me to step in and cover this class for the last few weeks of school."

A student in the back raised her hand. "What happened to Dr. Nottah?"

Mr. Faith pulled at his ear again, then replied, "Well, I'm not really at liberty to discuss the situation. Dr. Nottah, however, will continue as principal of the school. I will simply be in charge of this honors science class."

A boy near the front spoke out, "You know, you're the fourth teacher we've had this year. Like, why do they keep changing teachers on us?"

Mr. Faith put on his 'too big' smile and answered, "Really, I'm not at liberty to discuss that." Then, he picked up some handouts and said, "Well, now…um, I guess we should just go ahead and get started. Here is your final report assignment for the year. Let's look it over together."

After passing out the assignment, Mr. Faith continued, "Now, as you can see, your final report will cover how the 'bad design' of the natural things around us are evidence for evolution."

A boy with braces raised his hand. "Sir, if the driving force of evolution is survival of the fittest, why would bad design be evidence for evolution? I would think that natural selection or survival of the fittest would result in the *best* designs."

"Yes, yes," Mr. Faith nodded. "That is the 'end truth' of evolution. Over time, and time, and time, things become better suited through natural selection. However, we must remember that it has only been a few hundred million years since life really started evolving into complex organisms. And, mutations are not…um, well…always going to bring about the very best changes. Therefore, the fact that bad design exists proves that things are not yet 'finished'—they are still on their evolutionary road to 'perfection,' or, um, better fit, at least."

All 15 students in the class stared blankly back at Mr. Faith. Obviously, no understanding had been communicated.

"Okay," Mr. Faith licked his lips and tried again. "There are people who would contend that the perfect God made the natural world in six days. However, to believe this, you would have to believe that, from the first, God made everything just how He wanted it. That is to say, He made everything *perfect*—that is, good design—already *finished*."

"Yes," Jill spoke up. "It says in Genesis that after the six days of creation, God saw all that He had made, and it was 'very good.'"

"Yes, yes," Mr. Faith pulled at his earlobe. "I am familiar with that. After all, I go to church. I just don't believe that some things written in the Bible were meant to be believed, ummm, I mean, taken literally."

"What things?" David asked.

"Well, the story of creation," Mr. Faith answered. "And, the story of the Fall of Man. And, Noah's 'worldwide' Flood. And…"

"But, sir," Aaron questioned, "if you don't believe *those* parts of the Bible, why should you believe *any* part of the Bible?"

Mr. Faith stomped his foot and ran his fingers through his hair. "I do not want this to turn into a religious discussion! The point is this—if God created the world in six days, and it was very good, then everything should be perfect. Look around. Things are far from perfect (evidence against creation), but things are getting better and better, or at least, more fit (evidence for evolution)."

A girl in front responded, "My dad's a doctor, and he says that, from his perspective, things are getting *worse*! He says that more and more sicknesses, diseases, and genetic defects are around now-a-days than ever existed in the past."

While Mr. Faith thought this one through, David summarized, "Then, that would be evidence for the biblical explanation—at first, things were very good, but because of the Fall, things are getting worse…'groaning for the day of redemption.'"

"Mr. Avila!" Mr. Faith said in a stern voice, "I have stated that I do not want this to become a religious discussion!" Stomping his foot twice, he returned his attention to the report assignment. "Bad design is a *fact*. We see it everywhere."

"Where?" Jack challenged.

Mr. Faith answered with smug confidence, "Well, young man, just consider the human eye. Any engineer with a degree from any reputable college would have known better than to put the eye nerves in front of the retina. Why would an 'intelligent Creator' make such a flawed design? It makes more sense to say that God *used* evolution to create—this leaves room for such design weaknesses."

"So," Aaron verified, "you're saying that any good engineer could have designed the eye better than it is right now?"

"Yes, yes! Now I think you're beginning to see." Mr. Faith relaxed and sat down.

"Well," a boy with thick glasses in the second row cleared his throat, "if so many people could do a better job, then why am I sitting here wearing these dumb ol' glasses?"

"Yeah!" someone else spoke up. "I've heard that the very best, elite engineers can't come within 100 miles of making an eye as good as what we have now."

Mr. Faith stood up again. "Well, maybe the eye is too complicated of an example—too many details, and things you can't really understand. Instead, consider the rabbit—the family *Leporidae*. Now, talk about a poorly-designed digestive system…"

Jill giggled. "Are you saying that the critter that took over the whole continent of Australia in less than 50 years is poorly designed?"

"Skip Australia," a big farm boy in striped overalls said. "Just check out my back yard! We've tried shootin' em, trappin' em, and settin' the dogs on 'em. Still, last year, we only got about 15 green beans out of our five long rows. This year, my dad put up a fence!"

Pulling at both ears at once, Mr. Faith tried one last example. "Well, then, consider reproduction." All the students immediately got quiet. Many raised an eyebrow, wondering where their new teacher would go with this one.

Glad to have reclaimed their attention, Mr. Faith continued, "It is 100% obvious that asexual reproduction is, by far, more efficient than the need we see for male *and* female in almost all reproduction. I could go on and on and on about all the energy wasted, all the good genes compromised, and all the risks presented by normal reproduction. How can anyone call all that waste *very good*?"

The students stayed quiet, but most cocked their head to the side in a questioning manner. Finally, one of the more outspoken students asked, "Uh…Mr. Faith, are you married?"

"Yes, yes!" he nodded.

"And, you have children?"

"Yes, yes! Ginny and I have two boys and a girl—they are the joy of our life."

"And, you're still saying that the process necessary to produce these children, as well as the result (your children), was something other than *very good*."

Mr. Faith opened his mouth to respond but then quickly shut it. After a short pause, he threw back his head and laughed out loud. "No, no, no. I must admit that both the process and the results are very good." The students all snickered but were already beginning to like their new teacher.

"Okay," Mr. Faith said, wiping the tears of laughter from his very well-designed eyes. "You guys win. I give up. Just take your report assignment and do whatever you like with it."

*******

Up at the Maple Hill Cabin, David and Aaron talked with Billy about the debate the class had had with Mr. Faith.

Billy laughed loud and long when he heard the conclusion of the debate. But he had to sigh at how stubbornly folks held on to their evolutionary beliefs—even against the evidence. "I guess Jack hit it right on when he said that Mr. Justin Faith was holding on to evolution—*just in faith*."

David nodded. "Yeah, it was kind of frustrating. He said he goes to church, and he believes some of the Bible. But, he just kinda chooses what parts he wants to believe and doesn't believe the parts that don't fit his ideas about evolution.

"Well, keep in mind," Billy pointed out seriously, "that this is the state of much of the church today. Most people just don't realize what a dangerous game they're playing by picking and choosing what they do and don't want to believe from the Bible."

Suddenly, a loud and strange call came bursting out from the back room. "Yahoo-di-doo-di-doodle-doo!"

Everyone jumped up and ran to where Darin and Abel had been studying several dirt samples under the microscope. "We've found the match! We did it! The proof is in the scope! Take a look!" Darin waved Billy toward the microscope, then began his victory strut around the room while Abel hopped onto a bench, taking several elaborate bows for their job well done.

Once he was convinced that Darin had indeed found the missing piece to their geologic puzzle, Billy turned to slap the twins on the back. "Great work, you two!"

Aaron gave Darin a stinging high-five, while David shook hands with Abel. Then, Abel cleared his throat and put on his best reporter's voice as he began to interview Darin. "So, now, Dr. Genius, could you please explain the significance of your most recent find."

Darin first smoothed his hair and straightened his imaginary tie. Then, turning to smile into the non-existent camera, he said, "Through irrefutable scientific evidence, my partner and I have just verified the true identity of the mastermind and power source behind the anti-creation waves that have been crashing through Greenville. Her name is the one and only—Dr. Anita Moore-Power, President of Quantum Leap University."

# CHAPTER 14

Holding a tape player and notepad in her left hand, Cory used her right hand to check that her hair was all in place. Then, taking a deep breath, she pushed open the swinging door and stepped into the waiting room. The room was smaller than she had expected, but nice. There was a fish tank off to one side, as well as the usual waiting area magazines on a low table between two leather couches. On the far side of the room was the receptionist's desk. Cory approached the secretary with her well-rehearsed introduction. "Hi. My name is Corina Avila. I'm the journalist student from Clayton Community College. I have a 3:00 interview with President Moore-Power."

The secretary confirmed Cory's appointment on the computer, then stood to lead her into the president's office.

President Anita Moore-Power smiled as Cory entered her office. She advanced to shake her hand and showed her to a comfortable seat. "Hello Corina, I understand that you are working on an article about respected local women who hold positions of high authority."

"Yes, m'am," Cory answered, looking down at her interview notes. She bit her lip as she noticed the two really important questions about the debates buried in the midst of all the rest. She would have to be careful not to make those questions seem any more important than the others.

*******

After the interview, Dr. Moore-Power sat brooding at her desk. Her face was flushed, and her lips were pressed tight. Finally, she reached over and picked up her phone. Drake and Ellis would have to make sure that their motorcycle buddies would be free until the first of June. She had a job for them.

*******

Tiny downed a third beer and tossed the can into the weeds. He leaned back against a tree and slapped his thigh. "Whoo-wee! Big money's a-comin' this time!"

Bob nodded, but seemed more nervous than excited.

"What's the matter with you, man?" Tiny asked. "Don't you see? We've hit the *big time*! Money, money, money."

Bob nodded again. "Yeah, I know. But, if we get caught, we'll be in a whole heap of trouble, trouble, trouble."

"Hello!" Tiny reached over and knocked on the top of Bob's head. "I think you're missing the point here—m-o-n-e-y! Anyway, we'll be done in a few weeks. Then, if you're still too *lily-livered* to keep ridin' in the fast lane with me, you can take your part of the dough and just settle down with that Candy-chick like a pair of worthless goody-two-shoes."

Bob looked down at his feet. "Man, we ain't never *hurt* no one before."

Tiny grabbed another beer. "You ain't nothin' but a mama's boy. 'Course we've hurt people. You practically knocked Taylor's lights out just last week."

"That's different. Taylor done deserved it. Besides, he's a toughy, like us.

"Get over it, Bob. It's not like we're gonna kill nobody. Just...rough 'em up a little."

"Yeah, but, come on, they're just kids."

"Duh—they're kids. That's why them grown-ups are using them to do all their 'creation rant.' They know that this town don't wanna yell at no kids. That Billy James, Dr. Veritas, and Dr. Lution, they're smart dudes. What better way to get a town to give big money toward their museum than to get the kids all excited about it?"

Tiny paused to light up a smoke, then laughed to himself. "And, what better way to scare a whole town away from that there museum and all its creation talk than by startin' to rough up their kids?"

"Well, yeah, I guess, if you say so," Bob said, opening a beer. "Who we goin' after, anyhow?"

"First come, first serve..." Tiny quoted as he popped open the last beer.

"Um, then, did ya figure out how we're gonna make 'em think we was 'you-know-who'?" Bob asked, glancing nervously over his shoulder.

"You're a mama's boy *and* a scaredy-cat!" Tiny scoffed. "I only wish I had the Big Auger working with me to frame *you*, instead of the other way around. Big Aug weren't scared of nothin'."

"Yeah, well, what's he gonna think about us puttin' the rap on him?" Bob pressed.

"Ah, he ain't never gonna hear about it. Ya heard it for yerself. Sheriff Murphy and everybody says he's gone and left the state. No way is he gonna show his face 'round here for the next 100 years. You worry too much!" Tiny tossed his half-smoked cigarette at Bob. "All we have to do is leave the right clues ta convince the sheriff that Big Auger ain't so far away after all."

*******

When David and Cory got down on their hands and knees, Arby and Rax took the opportunity to make sure their faces were licked good and clean. Then they all headed into Tiger Cave.

Inside, the cave was well lit, and there was a rolled-up sleeping bag, a pillow, and stacks of library books along the wall. Big Aug looked up from a book and smiled as the teenagers crawled in. "I could smell somethin' good to eat comin' up the hill five minutes ago. Whatcha bring?"

Cory laughed and held up a large thermos bag. And David announced, "We brought Mama's Friday-night special—chicken with rice, corn muffins, spinach and cheese, and flan for dessert."

"Flan!" Aug raised both hands until they hit the ceiling. "Your mama's flan is my favorite food in the whole world!"

"Well, I guess you have *me* to thank for the two pieces I saved for you," Cory said in a saucy voice, "since David, here, was ready to devour it all—his, mine, and yours!"

Aug reached out a huge hand and swatted David on the arm. "Don't worry, man! When it comes to flan, it's every man for himself."

While Big Aug ate his dinner, David caught him up on what was going on. "Billy says that Dr. Nottah and Mr. Faith have finished rounding up a panel of eight qualified professors from QLU for the debate with Dr. Ted, Dr. Ed, and the rest of our Creation Science Club's team. That's set up, as planned, for June first at the museum's auditorium.

"He also talked with Sheriff Murphy, who said that he's been keepin' tabs on Tiny and Bob with the tracking units we stuck on their bikes. He said that they've mostly been hanging out at some old cabin by the creek. But," he added in a quieter voice, "each evening, they've been riding slowly down some back streets on *our* side of town."

Augustine looked up with his jaw tight, so Cory quickly spoke up in a cheerful tone. "My appointment with President Moore-Power went great! You should have seen her face when I asked her about her view of the creation/evolution debate planned for June first. She was absolutely stunned. It was hard not to laugh."

Aug relaxed and said, "I'll bet she was ready to spit fire."

"I wish I'd been there to see her," David laughed. "Also, Papa, Jill's uncle, and another professor have made an appointment with Judge John Bowers for this Monday to talk about how QLU's been spending its money. *And,* Mama's friend asked around at work and found out that the 'reliable source' that was blaming Dr. Ted and Dr. Ed for vandalizing their own museum was none other than the esteemed Dr. Jim Ellis, a current member of the QLU Board of Regents."

Big Aug smirked. "I told y'all that it was some schnooty-talkin' old guy. Anyway, sounds like things are goin' as planned. I just wish I could get outta this cave a little more. It's nice and cool in here, and I do like reading these books and all...but I guess my big ol' bones aren't made to be stuck in this hobbit hole."

"Then, you're gonna *love* what we have to tell you next," David said excitedly.

"What?" Aug asked, looking up from his meal.

David opened his mouth to explain, but Cory was so excited she jumped right in ahead of him. "Billy said one of his friends is flying up to Presque Isle tomorrow morning on business. He's agreed to fly Darin, Abel, Aaron, and Tasha with him. Billy said he'll take us—David, me, and you—in his plane."

"Sounds great!" Augustine smiled at her, but then added, "where on earth is Prisk Island?"

"Presque Isle," Cory corrected him gently, "is up on Lake Erie. It's not really an island. It's a peninsula that's attached to Erie, PA by a really skinny piece of land. That's why it's called Presque Isle, that means 'almost an island' in French."

"Wow," David said, "I didn't know that. But, I do know that it's like this beautiful little wildlife preserve that's surrounded by sandy beaches. You can hike through the woods, play on the beaches, or just hang out at the food-loaded concession stands."

"Sounds like heaven to me!" Aug laughed as he looked around the tiny cave he had been calling home. "Anyway," he added as he put his leftovers down for Arby and Rax to share, "we can feel pretty certain nobody's gonna recognize me out on some French-soundin' island way up on Lake Erie."

*******

The sun was shining in all its brilliance as the younger half of the Creation Science Club ran up the nature trail toward an area the ranger had said was "teaming with the new life of spring." Darin and Abel had stayed behind on the beach, surrounded by a group of kids, parents, and grandparents—all eager to hear the creation message from a pair of over-excited identical twins.

Billy and Big Aug strolled along a good 50 yards behind the teenagers, just enjoying the fresh air. Aug took a deep breath and let it out with a sigh of contentment. "Man, Billy, I guess I was born and bred to need the wilderness around me."

Billy agreed. "There are folks I meet that tell me they love the city life, but I've never quite believed 'em. I think they've just never had a chance to experience what the country has to offer."

"Well," Aug said casually, "they say it takes all kinds to make the world go 'round."

"Yep! God makes all kinds of folks!" Billy laughed as he took a stance that accented the obvious differences between himself and Big Aug. "But, no matter how a man is put together, God has made all of us with a plan and a purpose. I mean, I'm a man of decided likes—fresh air, good music, good friends, and spaces big enough to hold an adventure. But, with that said, I'll have to admit that I'll never be too far from where the people are. Nope. You see, inside of me is a call, a yearning to reach people with the truth, with the Gospel. In order to do that, I need to be where the people are. So, I guess God has given me a purpose that keeps me from turning 100% mountain-man."

Aug was quiet for a moment, then spoke in an earnest tone. "You know, it's because of the kindness of Miss Abbi and y'all that God called me outta my life of petty crime and the local taverns. I want to tell others about God's love, too. But," he shrugged his shoulders, "I know I'll never be no preacher, or fancy professor, or anybody that talks in front of all sorts of folks. I mean, who's gonna listen to me?"

"Augustine," Billy stopped and looked out toward the bay. "The Lord doesn't only use preachers and professors. He uses *any* godly man ready to reveal Him through his life and through his words. You know, God can use a factory worker just as well as a college professor."

"How 'bout a construction worker?" Aug asked, watching a long-legged bird run across the sandy soil.

Billy smiled. "God can use a construction worker just as well as anybody. The only condition is that you live a godly life."

Turning a corner in the path, the two men saw the others just ahead. They were all staring up into a tall tree through their binoculars.

"What are you all looking at?" Billy asked.

David handed Billy his binoculars, and Cory gave hers to Aug. About three-quarters of the way up the tree, and in near the trunk, were two large birds—very large.

"Awesome!" Aug whispered. "A pair of bald eagles."

"I think they're gonna nest here," Tasha said.

"Well," Billy answered, still viewing them through the binoculars, "maybe. But, this area is usually just a migration stop-over. I heard a couple of eagles did try to nest here some years back, but had to abandon their nest. And no eagles have tried since."

As everyone took turns with the binoculars, Big Aug started talking. "Did you know that eagles usually use the same nest year after year—they keep addin' to it each year. The nest can end up weighing *2,000 pounds* and be as big as a car. Bald eagles normally fly around 30 miles per hour. However, when diving, they can reach speeds over *100 miles per hour*. And, believe it or not, bald eagles can actually *swim*. They use an overhand movement of their wings that's a lot like the butterfly stroke used by human swimmers. This is a great help to them in catchin' fish. Ya know, fish are their main prey. And, amazingly, a *ten-pound* eagle can fly while holdin' an *eight-pound* fish. That'd be like Aaron, here, flyin' away with David. Not only that, but an eagle's eyes are so sharp that they can see between a mile and mile and a half away. They mate for life, and usually raise two eaglets a year."

By this time, everyone had lowered their binoculars and was staring open-mouthed at Big Aug. Augustine laughed at their expressions and explained, "I've got five books on bald eagles back at Tiger Cave."

"Hey, man!" Aaron said. "Can I borrow those books? I've just decided to include the bald eagle in my design report for Mr. Faith."

# CHAPTER 15

David hurried up the road toward the library. He and the gang were going to meet there and do some research. Then they would head on over to the museum for a meeting with the ever-growing Creation Science Club. Everyone was preparing for the big creation/evolution debate. As David passed the local barbershop, he couldn't help smiling about the latest news. Miss Eva Lution and her fiancé, Cliff Newman, were back in town. They had been talking with Dr. Ted and Miss Abbi, and had decided to have a double wedding. They had set the date for the 27th of June.

Passing the hardware store, David ducked into a narrow alley that led straight back to the library parking lot. He was still smiling about the double wedding when someone jumped him from behind. They fell to the ground together. David's arms were pinned, and the weight of his attacker knocked the breath clean out of him. Even after the man got up, he could hardly move. Then, while David lay groaning on the ground, his attacker snarled into his ear, "Listen, ya punk! You tell them friends of yers that the Big Auger is against anyone and everyone tryin' to open that there Creation Museum! Ya got that?"

David nodded. Then, the guy was gone. Sitting up, David touched his cheek, and his hand came away with blood on it. Then, he felt his ribs. They hurt. He sure wasn't smiling anymore.

*******

That Thursday evening, Aaron and Jack were walking into town for another meeting at the museum. Despite what had happened to David, the Club had continued to meet each evening to prepare for the debate. However, everyone was making sure to keep a sharp eye out for trouble.

The boys walked along at a fast pace and stuck close together. Everything seemed okay. But then, as they turned a corner at the back of one of the town's small churches, Aaron suddenly jumped back. Both Aaron and Jack turned to run, but it was too late. A big man grabbed at the boys and threw a blanket over their heads. Then, a smaller man ran toward them. Bob held the boys while Tiny lifted a pipe into the air, ready to put some serious bruises on their arms and legs.

*Slam!* Tiny and Bob found themselves pinned to the church wall by the rough hands of a giant. Augustine growled down into their faces, "To hurt and to maim was the Big Auger's favorite game…"

The color drained from Bob and Tiny's faces as they stared into the red eyes of the all-too-familiar silver bull head.

Tiny stammered, "H-h-hey, Big Aug, man, we don't w-w-want no trouble.

*Slam!* The two thugs hit the wall again. "Yer a liar, Tiny. I hate liars. If you ain't lookin' for trouble, why you carrying that heavy pipe?"

Tiny knew better than to answer Aug's question. He just let the pipe drop to the ground. With a last growl, Augustine pushed Bob and Tiny roughly away from him.

Bob and Tiny stumbled back a few steps, then turned and ran toward their motorcycles—hidden behind the church's dumpster. But, before they could reach them, Darin and Abel stepped into view waving a pair of wire snippers in the air. The bikes were now useless.

Spinning around, the two thugs saw Big Aug heading their way.

Tiny pulled out a knife and shouted, "Man, whatchu doin' in town, anyway?" Looking around for a way to escape, he added, "If you get caught after breaking out of the slammer, you could get 20 years."

"Now, what makes y'all so suddenly concerned about me," Big Aug snorted. "The way I see it, you've been leavin' muddy prints that lead back to me all along. Besides, who says I done broke outta any jail anyway?"

Bob answered, "We saw it on the news. Sheriff Murphy said you escaped out the window."

Big Aug laughed. "He also said that it was an inside job."

Tiny and Bob looked nervous and confused. "What you sayin', man?"

Abel came around to stand next to Augustine. "He's saying that the sheriff himself helped Aug 'escape' through the window. And, if you don't believe me, you can ask him yourselves, because here he is now."

As Abel spoke, Sheriff Murphy and a deputy came out from the church's back door. After what had happened to David, the sheriff had had someone on Bob and Tiny's tail every minute of the last few days.

When Tiny saw Sheriff Murphy, he lowered his knife and threw it to the ground.

*******

President Anita Moore-Power's face was grim as she watched the evening news on her 42-inch plasma TV from her calf-leather sofa.

The shot was of Jeane Jennings reporting live from the QLU campus. "President Moore-Power has stated that she is 'shocked' and 'tremendously disappointed' to hear that corruption has been discovered on the College Board of Regents."

Joe Power shook his head and rolled his eyes, but decided it was best not to say anything to his obviously angry wife.

The screen changed to a scene in front of Judge Bower's courthouse. Two well-dressed, older men and their lawyers were being led into the courthouse. Jeane Jennings explained, "Drs. James Ellis and Peter Drake were found to have been mishandling university funds for their own personal pleasure. Sheriff Shane Murphy reports that records have been found showing that $280 thousand have been embezzled from university accounts by these board members over the last two years."

The scene changed again, this time showing Bob and Tiny being arrested and handcuffed by Sheriff Murphy and the deputy. "Robert Ewing and Richard Temple were both arrested and charged with aggravated assault on a minor, as well as being charged with three counts of breaking and entering, two counts of malicious vandalism, one count of theft, and one count of arson. Sheriff Murphy has stated that Ewing and Temple were hired by Drs. Ellis and Drake to close down Greenville's newest attraction—Dr. Theodore Veritas' Creation Museum."

Jeane Jennings walked up to the QLU gateway, then turned to the camera. "Why were Ellis and Drake so set against Dr. Veritas's museum? Some say they were afraid that Greenville's interest in biblical creation might cause the people to hesitate in voting for a levy that would give millions of tax dollars to QLU. We can only guess that Ellis and Drake were depending on that tax money to cover their addiction to nice cars and fancy clothes. Phil Lovit has more on the story."

Anita Moore-Power growled to herself and bit off one of her $80 false nails when the TV screen filled with a shot of Dr. Ted's museum.

Phil's smiling face filled the screen. "Phil Lovit here, live, down by Greenville's future Creation Science Museum. Now, as you look around at all the people going in and out of the museum, you might think that it's already open to the public. However, all these people are just volunteers. Yes, many of the people who have been following the trials of this little museum are now volunteering their time to make sure this museum will be ready to open early next fall."

As Phil entered the museum itself, he continued, "While the museum is presently enjoying widespread popularity, they continue to exercise caution. They've installed security locks and silent alarms, as well as hidden surveillance cameras. And, if those aren't enough, check this out..." Phil approached a very large, young man dressed in a nicely pressed uniform. "And, who, sir, are you—a linebacker or a pro wrestler?"

The man chuckled and bent down to talk into the microphone. "My name's Augustine. I'm the new security guard here at the museum. I'm here to make sure nobody causes any more trouble."

Phil smiled at the camera. "Well, Augustine, I certainly think Dr. Veritas and Dr. Lution picked the right man for the job."

Jeane Jennings was now standing in front of the QLU science building. "Now, those of you who have been following the progress of the museum might also be interested in attending the upcoming creation/evolution debate to be held at Dr. Veritas's Carmel Street Museum. There will be eight highly-qualified scientists from QLU taking an evolutionary stand against eight scientists who believe the biblical account of creation. This debate will be held on June first at 7:00 p.m."

*Crash!* Anita Moore-Power threw the remote with all her strength toward the TV screen. It bounced off the panel, and the TV went blank.

# CHAPTER 16

**The Human Eye**
**(A Bad Design?)**
by David J. Avila

## Introduction

Many evolutionary resources (textbooks, museums, websites, etc.) claim that 'vestigial organs' and 'bad design' are clear evidence for evolution. They reason that no Creator would include useless vestigial organs (like the human appendix) or poorly designed organs (like the human eye) in His creation. This evidence, they claim, clearly supports evolution's random processes working over millions of years with no plan, no purpose, and no design.

Creation, however, claims the exact opposite—that all things were created by God with an amazing plan, for a clear purpose, and show incredible design. For this report, I will look at the most up-to-date evidence in order to show that 'vestigial organs' are not useless—as evolutionists want us to think. Then, I will look at one of evolution's favorite examples of 'bad design' (the human eye) and show that it simply *cannot* be explained by evolution's random, chance processes. The human body, from head to toe, is overwhelming evidence for design—revealing the glory of the Creator.

**Vestigial Organs?**

At one time, evolutionists claimed that there were over 180 useless, vestigial structures in the human body. Vestigial organs are parts of the body that evolutionists claim have no function—calling them 'useless evolutionary leftovers.' Examples from this list include the appendix, tonsils, tail-bone, and wisdom teeth. Evolutionists claim that each item on their long list is repeated evidence that humans evolved. They reason that no Creator would include over 180 useless parts in its 'design' for a human.

In recent years, however, important uses have been found for almost all of these 'vestigial organs.' The appendix is a good example. Many scientists once considered the appendix to be a useless evolutionary leftover—after all, we can easily live without it. They explained that the appendix did, at one time, have a use in one of our evolutionary ancestors. But, since we have evolved, we no longer need an appendix.

But, new studies have found that the appendix *does* have functions, such as controlling bacteria and fighting infection in the intestines. And, just because we can live without an appendix doesn't make it useless. I mean, we can live without our eyes, but that certainly doesn't make *them* useless.

Just as with the appendix, scientists are continually finding real, important uses for nearly all of the so-called 'vestigial organs' on evolution's long list. So, the 'vestigial organ' argument itself seems to have become a useless evolutionary leftover.

**Bad Design?**

Evolutionists claim that design 'flaws' are further proof that all living things are the result of evolution's 'blind' random chance, rather than the result of planned design. One of their favorite examples of 'flawed' design is the human eye—specifically, its 'backwardly' wired retina. You see, the nerves of the eye are connected to the front of the retina (where the visual image forms) instead of to the back. Evolutionists say that these nerves interfere with the image, just like running a power cord in front of a data projector would interfere with the image on the screen. They claim it would make better sense for the nerves to be connected to the back of the retina so that they are completely out of the way.

However, if we look at things from a different perspective, the 'backwardly' wired retina makes perfect sense. This is because there are some very important parts already located behind the retina. There is the choroid, which supplies all the blood needed for the retinal pigment epithelium (RPE). And, there is the RPE, which is needed to regenerate the photoreceptors. It's this constant regeneration of photoreceptors that makes it possible for us to see. The RPE also absorbs excess heat—keeping the eye from 'burning out.' So, it's actually *necessary* for the nerves to go in front of the retina instead of behind it. On top of this, the nerves are very small and almost transparent, so they don't really interfere with the visual image anyway.

Evolutionists also claim that the 'blind spot' resulting from where the nerves actually connect to the retina is a serious problem. But this blind spot takes up less than one percent of the field of vision. And, this blind spot is located far away from the center of vision. So, in reality, the blind spot is no problem at all. What evolutionists have called 'flawed' is, in reality, an exceptionally well-thought-out design.

By spending their time looking for the 'flaws,' evolutionists have totally missed seeing what a masterpiece of incredible design the human eye really is. Just think, the eye has amazing color perception, excellent resolution, and can handle an incredibly huge range of light intensity—being able to detect one *single* photon of light, or being able to handle the intensity of 10 *billion* photons. Not even the latest digital cameras can come even close to handling the light intensity that the human eye can handle. And, no one would claim that a digital camera is the result of blind, random chance rather than design. But this is exactly what evolutionists are claiming concerning the eye. If you look at the evidence, the incredible design of the human eye definitely points to a Creator.

**Evolution's Story?**

The QLU website uses a costly computer simulation to show us how they believe the human eye evolved. The simulation starts with Darwin's idea that the eye began as a light-sensitive spot on the surface of the skin of some distant ancestor. Then, over generations, the light-sensitive layer bends gradually into a cup shape. Over millions of years, it continues to curve until it's a hemisphere filled with a clear liquid. Next, the outside ends close in together forming a ball-shape. Then, the transparent cover gradually changes into a focusing lens. Finally, after hundreds of millions of years of mistakes, you have the amazing human eye.

The animation of this simulation is top quality, but where is the scientific evidence to back up the theory? Just because scientists believe the eye evolved, and then design a computer program showing the eye evolve, doesn't prove anything. (Remember, the program was created by intelligent people—not by random chance).

In reality, there is very little *biological* evidence to support the belief in eye evolution. There *are* organisms with light-sensitive cells. And there *are* an incredible variety of eyes among various animals. But there are *no* examples of transitional forms of a light-sensitive spot changing into any of the variety of eyes that exist today.

Evolutionists believe in evolution. Therefore, they must believe that eyes evolved from nothing into the incredible variety of eyes that there are today—even though it goes against the evidence. And so, they use professional computer simulations (rather than evidence) to try and convince us to believe it, too.

**Conclusion**

Many evolutionary resources are *still* claiming that 'vestigial organs' and 'bad design' are clear evidence for evolution. They say that these so-called 'useless' and 'poorly designed' organs clearly support evolution's random processes working over millions of years with no plan, no purpose, and no design. But, modern scientists have found important uses for almost all of evolution's 'vestigial organs.' And, a modern understanding of how the human eye works shows that evolution's claim that it represents 'bad design' with some 'serious flaws' is really just a 'bad argument' with some 'serious misconceptions.'

Creation, on the other hand, claims that all things were created by God with an amazing plan, for a clear purpose, and showing incredible design. The human body *cannot* be explained by evolution's random, chance processes. The fact is, even if you gathered a team of the world's most elite scientists and gave them an endless supply of resources, they couldn't even begin to design something as wonderful and amazing as the human body. The evidence (all living things) speaks for itself—to the glory of the Creator. "I praise you [God] because I am fearfully and wonderfully made; your works are wonderful, I know that full well" (Psalm 139:14).

* * * * * * *

The velociraptor fixed its steely gaze on the young triceratops. Step by step the dragon advanced, stopping occasionally to raise its head and sniff the air. There was no sign of the farmer that had saved the foolish little dinosaur the last time he had escaped his fence. This time, he would *not* get away. Baby-back ribs were on the menu tonight!

After taking another step, the predator paused, looking at the ground beneath it. It seemed as if the ground was starting to shake. Then came a crashing sound. Raising itself to its full height, the dragon looked farther into the woods. Immediately, it opened its mouth wide and screamed, "Hey, no fair!" Running toward the dragon, with horns lowered, was an entire herd of triceratops. The beast spun around and took off at top speed. However, the chase was short, ending with the velociraptor making a leaping dive into the ErinWood pond.

Coming up out of the water, Darin complained to Abel, "You're a cheater-cheater-boom-ba-leater! You set me up! I didn't even know all the others were here!"

Abel and Aaron high-fived, while David and Jack did their own version of Darin's now-famous victory strut. Cory, Tasha, and Jill just laughed and threw the early summer flowers at Darin as he sludged his way out of the pond.

At this point, Billy and Carmen strolled up arm-in-arm shaking their heads at Darin's dripping figure. "Hey, Darin, you'd better get changed," Billy called. "Dinah and Rebekah just called from the airport. And, I thought after workin' so hard to get your license, you might like to be the one to go pick 'em up."

Darin's pouty face instantly changed to an expression of lovesick joy. With a whoop and a holler, he was off to the James' cabin to change.

David laughed and turned to Billy. "I'm glad the Soures can make it for the wedding…I mean, *weddings*."

Mrs. Carmen smiled. "Dinah has made quite an e-mail friendship with both Eva and Abbi. And, of course, Bekah wouldn't want to disappoint Darin. But," she added, "Terry and Stego are going to stay in Argentina to get some work done, and then they'll meet us all in Seattle."

Tasha reached down to pick a lily. "I am, like, so totally excited that our Creation Science Club was chosen to go on the Christian cruise line's 'practice' cruise to Alaska." Then, she put the flower behind her ear as she remarked, "I think a week 'almost' alone on a brand new cruise ship will be the perfect honeymoon for the newlyweds—don't you think so?" she asked Abel, as she put her arm through his and led him off for a walk around the pond.

Cory watched as Tasha and Abel walked off together. "Is Big Aug coming too?" she asked with a blush, as she carefully put a lily behind her own ear.

"Yep!" Billy said with a chuckle.

Some kind of sudden understanding seemed to dawn on David as he looked at the blush on his sister's face. "Now, wait just a minute…" he started to say in a protective tone.

But Aaron and Jack just laughed and started to push him around while they sang, "The stallion and his mare, the rabbit and his hare; love is a mystery that's always near. The bull and his cow, the boar and his sow; love is a mystery that's happening right now."

Mrs. Carmen winked at Cory and said, "I think maybe we'll have to change this cruise ship's name to the 'Love Boat.'"

Cory tossed her head at their teasing, but looked pleased as she headed up to the cabin.

# A NOTE FROM DAVID

Hola Compañeros!

Through this latest adventure, I personally learned a lot about not judging people too quickly. I mean, no one, except for God, can see into a person's heart.

Big Aug is a tough guy with a history of trouble. But, when Miss Abbi showed him a little bit of kindness, we got to know him as an honest and loyal friend. And, Dr. Chance sure was defensive and grumpy at first. But, when our gang treated him with genuine respect, God opened the door for real communication.

At the beginning of the year, I felt like I just wanted to 'show all those evolutionists that they were wrong.' But my dad helped me to see that it's never right to tear another person down even when they believe differently than you. God's command is that we "love one another."

So, when I debate with others about creation and evolution things, I try to keep God's love as my number one goal.

En el amor de Dios,
David

# ABOUT THE AUTHORS

John is a nationally certified middle school teacher. He has worked with teenagers for the past 20 years, both as a teacher and as a youth pastor. Lisa received her college degree in English Literature. She has also been active working with youth for the past 20 years. The Foxes live on a ten-acre farm in Central Ohio where they homeschool their six children. They also own lots of dogs and a variety of fun farm animals.

**Authors' Note**

Although this book is a work of fiction, the scientific evidence discussed is *real* and is available to everyone. Evolution's bold 'scientific' claims have clear religious implications against faith in God and His Word. Our goal is simply to provide real scientific evidence that refutes evolution's claims and upholds the Word of God from beginning to end. We encourage our readers to ask questions and to do further research.

And, always remember that we are *not* looking for evidence to *prove* the Bible. We believe that the Bible is true. Therefore, we believe that God's Word is the best foundation for understanding *all* the science we discover in the world and in the universe.

## RECOMMENDED RESOURCES:

### THE CREATION ANSWERS BOOK

*The Creation Answers Book* provides biblical answers to over 60 important questions that everyone wants to know about creation/evolution and the Bible like "What about dinosaurs, carbon 14 dating, and who was Cain's wife?". Not only will it answer your questions, but it will equip you to effectively respond to the questions of others. This important work is a 'must have' for anyone's library.

### WHAT THE SCHOOLS ARE TEACHING DVD

Have you ever wondered what textbooks are teaching about living things, as opposed to what the Bible teaches? It should not surprise you that they are opposites, but it might surprise you that the textbooks contain outright falsehoods. Learn to spot the lies so you can help your family, train up church youth, and answer the unbelieving world.

### EVIDENCE FOR CREATION

This booklet presents evidence from astronomy, geology, biology, and history to show why Darwin's theory is at odds not just with Genesis, but with the facts of science itself. Discover why the fossil record, physical laws, and cellular complexity support creation, not evolution. Also, see why grim social consequences follow when political leaders embrace evolution. Be prepared for challenging, intelligent answers.

## COMIC BOOKS

'Everybody reads comics'—so, what a great way to reach youth and old alike. Beautifully illustrated and full of information, these are great booklets to give to those who may shun the conventional creationist material. Each closes with a powerful salvation message.

## CHRISTIANITY FOR SKEPTICS

This updated classic answers key questions like: Does God exist? Why is there evil? Is the Bible the Word of God? What about other religions, including Islam and the New Age? It also contains cutting-edge material on design in nature and the Christian roots of science. Ideal to place in the hands of a skeptical friend, family member, or co-worker.

## BUSTING MYTHS: 30 PH.D. SCIENTISTS WHO BELIEVE THE BIBLE AND ITS ACCOUNT OF ORIGINS

See why specialists in astronomy, biology, chemistry, genetics, geology, and physics affirm that science supports a straightforward reading of Genesis, and why they believe that evolution contradicts both science and Scripture.

CREATION.com

For more information on creation/evolution and Bible-science issues


**AUSTRALIA**
*Creation Ministries International (Australia)*
PO Box 4545
Eight Mile Plains, QLD 4113

**Phone:** (07) 3340 9888
**Fax:** (07) 3340 9889
ABN 31 010 120 304

**CANADA**
*Creation Ministries International (Canada)*
300 Mill St, Unit 7
Kitchener, ON N2M 5G8

**Phone:** (519) 746–7616
**Orders & donations:** 1-888-251-5360
**Fax:** (519) 746–7617

**NEW ZEALAND**
*Creation Ministries International (NZ)*
PO Box 39005
Howick, Auckland 2145

**Phone/Fax:** (09) 537 4818
A Registered Charitable Trust

**SINGAPORE**
*Creation Ministries International (Singapore)*
Clementi Central Post Office
PO Box 195
Singapore 911207

**Phone:** 9698 4292

**SOUTH AFRICA**
*Creation Ministries International (SA)*
PO Box 3349
Durbanville 7551

**Phone:** (021) 979 0107
**Fax:** (086) 519 0555

**UK & Europe**
*Creation Ministries International (UK/Europe)*
15 Station St,
Whetstone, Leicestershire, LE8 6JS

**Phone:** 0116-2848-999

**USA**
*Creation Ministries International (USA)*
PO Box 350,
Powder Springs, GA 30127

**Phone:** (800) 616-1264
**Fax:** (770) 439-9784

**OTHER COUNTRIES**
*Creation Ministries International*
PO Box 4545
Eight Mile Plains,
QLD 4113, Australia

**Phone:** +617 3340 9888
**Fax:** +617 3340 9889